THE COLD FEE
MOTHER GR
PA

Officer Jack Kreevitch found the park ranger's body almost immediately. It was in the bushes and not in the water, so at least they didn't have to drag the canal for him.

Shot in the head. Right here in Fishersville. *God damn,* he thought, *this town is getting really dangerous.* If a ranger could get himself shot in the middle of a Saturday afternoon, no one in town was safe. Kreevitch himself wasn't safe. He looked around, but he didn't see anyone.

Clumsy hunters? Snipers? Kids? One man shot in the head on the canal bank might have been a tragic coincidence, but two in the same week. . . .

He radioed headquarters. More work for the county prosecutor's office.

Trying not to disturb the crime scene, Kreevitch looked around for clues. But the integrity of the crime scene was a joke; the rain was coming down in torrents now, obliterating everything. If there ever was a clue to be found, it would be gone, washed into the canal. . . .

UNHOLY ANGELS

A
Mother Lavinia Grey
Mystery

*Kate
Gallison*

A DELL BOOK

Published by
Dell Publishing
a division of
Bantam Doubleday Dell Publishing Group, Inc.
1540 Broadway
New York, New York 10036

ISBN: 0-440-22220-6

Printed in the United States of America

Published simultaneously in Canada

September 1996

10 9 8 7 6 5 4 3 2 1

1

Fishersville, New Jersey, greasy river town turned tourist mecca, stretches long and thin between the bank of the Delaware River to the west and steep cliffs of black rock to the east. Through the town from north to south runs the Delaware and Raritan Canal Feeder, and alongside the feeder the town's latest improvement, the state bike trail.

Locals on foot use this trail for a shortcut to the Acme and the Little League ball field, since the park runs the length of the town and beyond, and also for a dog bathroom (when they can do so unobserved). Tourists, for whom it was intended, use it for a north-south bicycle road, although the ballsy still scorn death and take the narrow highway, heedless of gravel trucks. Ducks and geese use the trail as a place to raise their families. On a certain summer morning Mother Lavinia Grey, the vicar of St. Bede's

Episcopal Church, was trying out the D & R Canal bike trail as a place of healthful exercise.

Years had passed since she last rode a bicycle, but what with her parish duties and her efforts at social action, there was no time for hiking in the mountains anymore, and though she was only thirty-seven, the pounds were creeping on. Two weeks ago her size-six secondhand Episcopalian gray wool suit had refused to button. The doctor said, "Thirty minutes of exercise, three times a week, Mother Vinnie."

Her friend Sheila said, "I'll sell you my bicycle."

"If it works out, I'll buy it from you," she replied, and so here she was wobbling unsteadily toward a gaggle of Canada geese, two parents and five fuzzy yellowish goslings. The big ones stretched their necks at her and moved off the trail, and the goslings waddled after them on enormous feet.

Towser was not there to chase them. Rules about dog behavior on the trail were posted everywhere on signs bearing a cartoon dog making dog doo inside a circle-and-slash symbol. Afoot, she could leash her dog and pick up after him, but not on a bicycle, so she left him home. Leaves weighed down the boughs of the young trees and swatted her in the face. She found it hard enough to control this wobbling bicycle without having to worry about rowdy canines.

A mallard duck mother led a string of peeping babies to the canal and glided in. All the young of the town were out this morning; around the corner came four boys on bicycles, serious-faced, breathing hard, pedaling steadily.

She knew them all: two of the Reeker brothers,

Garrett Hudson, and her young friend and parishioner Freddy Kane. The Reekers were hard to miss: ears and faces pierced and festooned with gold jewelry, hair grotesquely abused. Chick's coiffure was partly shaved and partly long and flowing, Howie's trained into spikes with fluorescent blue goo. Freddy still wore his hair neatly trimmed in a mushroom cut, no rings in his nose or diamonds in his ears, but then he was not yet an adolescent.

Garrett Hudson, who pitched for Freddy's baseball team, wore no jewelry either; the coaches frowned on earrings and nose-piercing. To be cool he wore his clothes baggy, his pants low, and his baseball cap back to front, like Freddy's.

As they pulled up to let her pass, Mother Grey smiled and wished them good morning. Only Freddy returned her greeting. He looked oddly abashed, almost as if she had caught him up to no good. She wondered fleetingly what Freddy was doing with those bigger boys, a possible bad influence.

Freddy cast an eye after Mother Grey the way a sailor setting forth on a stormy sea might gaze at the receding lights of the harbor. Then he turned and followed the big boys, past the backyards of Fishersville's close-packed houses, past the lumberyard, over the tracks of the tourist railroad. They pedaled hard, nobody speaking. The only sound came from their whizzing bicycle tires and their panting breath.

"Are you sure these people aren't home?" Freddy said. House burglary was not something he ordinarily got into. The most he had ever stolen before this was a pack of gum from the supermarket, and when his mom found out, she whipped him.

"Shut up, kid," Chick Reeker said.

"They're all out of there," Garrett Hudson said. "Old man Todd, his son, and all three of the dogs. Gone to the ball field for their free rabies shots. Don't worry, we won't let them catch you." It was going to be Freddy's job to get in first through a small opening in the house and unlock the doors.

"We hid behind a bush and watched them get in the station wagon," Howie said.

Howie hid behind a bush? "They didn't notice your blue spikes sticking up?" Freddy said.

"Nah. I ducked down really low. Then I personally followed them to the field and watched them get out," he said. "There's a long line of dogs in front of them. We should have lots of time."

Garrett checked his watch. "Twenty minutes anyway," he said. "Let's get busy." They stopped at a crude barricade bearing a hand-lettered sign that said NO TRESPASSING, THIS MEANS YOU. "It's right up ahead," Garrett said. "We can leave the bikes here."

"Hope they remember to get a rabies shot for the old man," said Chick. "Dirty dog that he is."

"Why does everyone hate him?" Freddy asked.

"Stinking developers," said Chick. "Everyone hates 'em. They build stuff, so more people move into town. The new people park their cars on our street, my mother can't find a parking place, and we have to carry her groceries three blocks."

"Oh."

"Also he chases women," Howie said.

"We don't talk about that," Garrett said.

"Right, right," Howie said.

"What he mainly does, and also the reason we're here," Garrett said, "is he collects guns."

"And threatens people with them," Howie said. "So he needs to be relieved of the collection."

"Which is where we come in," said Chick. "But we told you all that. Now be quiet."

They had told him, or Garrett had told him, that the man who lived here said he was going to shoot anybody who used the bike trail beside his house. The police wouldn't do anything because he hadn't actually fired at anyone. He might start anytime, though, Garrett had told him, as long as he had all those guns. The thing to do was to steal them while everybody was out of the house, Bunker Todd, his son, Randy, and the three ugly Rottweilers. For the good of the town, of course.

They needed Freddy's help because he was small.

Freddy had never completely bought Garrett's story; he figured Garrett and the Reekers wanted Mr. Todd's guns to play with. But Freddy needed a gun very seriously, and so he had agreed to come along and help.

Freddy's stepfather was back in town.

He had seen him killed, had personally helped to throw his body in the river, and yet one day last winter Freddy picked up the phone and heard Rex Perskie's voice, calling from who knows where, trying to reverse the charges. Soon afterward he thought he saw Rex's hairy face scowling in at him through his own bedroom window, two stories up.

It might have been a dream, or not. Maybe Rex could float in the air. Maybe he was undead.

So Freddy had to start thinking about protecting himself, protecting his mother, now that her new husband, Ralph, was away all the time, driving a truck. He needed a real gun, even if he had to steal one.

The house they were going to rob stood by the side of the bike trail, shaded by old trees, surrounded by wild ducks and geese. The geese hissed at them when they approached the house and then began to honk, noisier than barking dogs. No other houses were near; there was no one to hear and raise the alarm. "Okay, Freddy," Garrett said. "Do your thing."

A special door let the dogs go in and out of the Todds' basement, too small for the bigger boys to fit through but just right for Freddy, or so they all assured him. "Go on," they said. "If you get stuck we'll pull you out. We won't leave you."

Stuck? He thought about getting stuck in the Rottweilers' door, leaving them free to gnaw on whatever part of his body they came to first, outdoors or in.

He exhaled, squeezed through the narrow opening, and plunged down a muddy ramp into the dark space that was the Todds' cellar. It reeked of dog stink. Suddenly he was sure the big boys had lied about seeing them leave. The Rottweilers were still there, waiting for him. He could almost feel their breath, feel their wicked eyes on him. Garrett and the others were out there having a good laugh, waiting to hear him get chewed to pieces.

But no. When his eyes adjusted to the gloom, he saw that there were no dogs down here, only the usual basement clutter. A black outline of stairs appeared, leading up through the grayness of the basement ceiling.

Up he went. The door into the Todds' kitchen was closed but not locked; from there it was a simple matter to find the front door and let the other boys in.

The Reekers ran inside and raced up to the second floor.

"You be the lookout," Garrett said, and he rushed to the back of the house. "I think the guns are down here."

"Lookout," Freddy repeated. He went to the window and looked out, at the green trees and bushes, the empty doghouses, the empty driveway. He strained his ears for the barking of Rottweilers or the crunch of tires on gravel. *Run away, run away,* said his mind, but his body stood still while the others crammed things into trash bags. He heard thumping, glass breaking, drawers falling on the floor.

"Here they are! We got 'em!" It was Howie, upstairs.

"All right, let's go!" Garrett called.

He meant it like an order to soldiers, but more like crazy thieves they rushed through the front door, getting in each other's way. The geese started their noise again.

Someone said, "I hear them coming."

They leaped on their bikes and headed south, the green bags bumping over their shoulders. They never stopped pedaling until they were entirely out of breath, far beyond the Acme, almost all the way to the ball field. Then they threw their bikes and the trash bags into the bushes and fell down to rest.

When he got his breath back, Garrett opened the bag of guns and spread the contents out on the weeds.

"Where's the AK-47?" he said. "I heard he had an AK-47 and a couple of nine-millimeter semiautomatics."

"These are all I could find," said Howie.

"They're nothing but target pistols." Garrett made a face. "Twenty-two caliber."

"They're still real guns, right? You could still shoot somebody with them," Howie said.

"Yeah, but they're wimpy," Garrett said.

Chick picked up the biggest, a black automatic. "This one is mine, okay?"

"I'm taking this one," Garrett said, selecting a long-barreled revolver. "Which one do you want, Freddy?"

"Why can't I have two guns? You guys couldn't have got in there without me."

"Sorry, kid. You only get one," Garrett said.

"Why? There are five here."

"Our brother has a buyer in Trenton for one of them," Chick said. "So we get three, Garrett gets one, and you get one."

"Give me the little one, then."

Garrett handed Freddy the small revolver. It was

8

like a short cowboy gun, smooth, cold, and shiny. His cello case had a pocket inside that would just hold it, where his mother would never look. When Rex came, he would be ready.

"Hey, Freddy, where's your hat?"

"My hat?"

"Your Angels hat. I thought you had it on earlier."

"Oh, yeah. I did." He put his hand up to his head, feeling the cobwebs and cellar grit in his hair. "I guess it came off someplace."

"Is your name in it?"

"No. I haven't had to put my name in my team hat since I was in tee-ball. Nobody fools with my hat."

"The cops might find it, if it came off in the Todds' cellar," said Chick.

"So what?" said Freddy. "My name isn't in it." But maybe his fingerprints were on it or something. Or bits of his hair. He would have to be real careful not to let the cops take bits of his hair or get his fingerprints from now on.

A voice called in the distance, high and singsong: "Garrett!"

Garrett grabbed the nearest bag. "It's my stupid sister. My mother must have sent her to get me. Let's get out of here." Frantically Garrett and the Reekers stuffed bullets and cigarette packs into various openings in their clothing.

"Your sister is such a hot babe," said Chick Reeker.

"Yeah, right," said Garrett. "If you like pain."

The voice called again, getting closer. "Garrett! Where are you, you little dork?"

They plunged into the bushes. Freddy stuck the revolver into the waistband of his pants and adjusted his shirt to hang down over it. For a moment he would have followed the others, running like a thief, but he thought, *No. I'm not doing anything wrong.* The others might be robbers, but he was a noble hero defending his mother. With every appearance of calm he got back on his bike and started home along the trail.

Soon Dawn Hudson came jogging toward him. A hot babe? Was that what a hot babe looked like? It was true that you could see a lot of her skin, the way she was dressed, and you could say she was pretty. But Freddy had heard how she bullied Garrett, how she messed with his stuff, took his money, and beat him up. If that was what hot babes were all about, then he didn't want any part of them.

Dawn the hot babe was jogging right up the middle of the trail, so that he had to brake to get around her safely. She looked up and noticed him. Her eyes were painted with black stuff.

"Hey, Freddy!" she said. "Have you seen Garrett?"

"Garrett?" he said.

"You just came from my brother," she said. She grabbed the handlebars of his bike and shook them, so that he had to get off or fall off. "Tell me where he is."

"I don't know where he is."

She got hold of the top of his shirt and pulled

him so close he was afraid she would notice the gun in his waistband. Her breath stank of violet gum.

"I know where you live, you little bastard. If you're lying to me, you're dead meat."

2

Most people in town knew nothing of the gun robbery, even days later, since the daily papers hadn't covered it and the weekly *Clarion* wasn't out yet. As far as Mother Grey knew, the worst thing the youth of the town had done lately was to write bad words in green crayon on the steps of her rectory while waiting for the school bus.

All traces of this activity must be removed before next week, when she was expecting a visit from representatives of the Diocesan Department of Missions, maybe even the Archdeacon himself, to check on how she was doing, to check on whether it was time yet to close down St. Bede's. She set to work scrubbing. Everybody in the diocese had seen the old F-word before, some of them probably used it in ordinary conversation, but it would look bad to the Archdeacon scrawled on the steps of the priestly residence. It would look almost like a rejection by the community of her mission here at St. Bede's.

Because her mission here was always tenuous. Four years ago, when the bishop sent her to close the church, Mother Grey had found the lovely old building in ruins and the parishioners elderly and few. By using St. Bede's as a base for much-needed social programs, she had managed to keep it going—barely—as little by little her flock increased.

She thought the diocese would surely force her to close the church the time the old rectory burned down. Thanks be to God they let her use the insurance money to buy this place, with its concrete front stoop. Horace Burkhardt, the kindly old man who sold it to her at such a reasonable price, lived in the house next door now. He seemed to own half the town; she was always hearing of some fresh chunk of Fishersville real estate that belonged to him. Last week at Delio's luncheonette somebody said he owned the Little League ball field.

Another three or four minutes of this, and the crayon would surely be gone from these steps. She scrubbed harder. A shadow fell across her work. She looked up, pushing the hair out of her eyes with her forearm, and saw a tall, slim black man in jeans and a baseball jacket. His skin was the color of mahogany. He looked like somebody, some famous African-Hollywood movie star whose name she couldn't remember.

"Excuse me," he said. "Are you Mother Lavinia Grey?" His voice was deep and resonant.

"Yes, I am."

"My name is MacLeod Barrow. Do you have a minute, or is this a bad time?"

"No, it's fine. How do you do, Mr. Barrow?" She wiped the suds off on her jeans and extended her hand, which he took in his own warm, dark hand, applying the correct degree of friendly pressure.

"Call me Mac," he said.

She stood back and looked at the steps. The writing seemed to be gone, though she would have to check it later when the step was dry. "How can I help you?" she said.

"They tell me St. Bede's has a Hook and Hastings tracker organ."

"It's not in the best of repair, I'm afraid." The hundred-year-old pipe organ had been mute for a generation; no one but Mother Grey had gone near it since she came to St. Bede's to be vicar. She had started it up and tried to play it herself a couple of times, but she was no keyboard musician. Even so, she could tell that the thing was in terrible shape.

"Would you like someone to play it on Sunday mornings?"

Who was this man? Why was he carrying on about St. Bede's organ? He was dressed like a baseball player, in athletic shoes and a nylon Angels jacket that said COACH on the pocket. "I would have to think about it," she said. "Who did you have in mind?"

"Me," he said, grinning. "I can direct your choir too."

Could it be? Ever since she had come to St. Bede's, she had prayed for someone to play that organ. Sung masses, choir anthems, hymns in four-part harmony with everybody on pitch. Gorgeous organ preludes rolling forth as the church filled up before services. In her dreams. "We can't pay you anything," she said.

"No problem. I'll do it for nothing for six months."

"And then?"

He had a very engaging smile. "Then the church will be packed every Sunday, and you can afford to pay me. We'll renegotiate."

"You can really play the organ?" A small worm of mistrust gnawed at her vitals. Something was wrong with this. Why would he want to play the organ for nothing? It was true that she needed an organist, even more true that there was no money. But . . .

"I studied keyboard at Westminster Choir College. Actually I'm on the faculty there now, teaching voice."

"No kidding," she said. In her mind she took the baseball jacket off him and replaced it with a choir robe. It seemed to fit. A handsome fellow. A choir director! She considered the singing voices of her tiny congregation. Could she scrape four parts together?

"If you'll let me have a key to St. Bede's, I can get in and practice sometimes, maybe do a little minor repair work."

The worm took another nibble. The last person with a key to the church had used it to break in and bury body parts. Was MacLeod Barrow some sort of con man? He was handsome and charming enough to do very well at it. She would test him.

"I have some friends at the choir college," she said. "Do you know Jane Bussey?"

"I know her slightly. A nice lady, and a fine singer."

Okay, he seemed to know who Jane Bussey was. But did he know one end of a pipe organ from the other?

"Would you like to have a look at the old Hook and Hastings?" she said. "Poor thing, it needs quite a bit of work."

"I'd love to see it."

She unlocked the side entrance to the sacristy, and they stepped inside, into a faint mist of old incense and beeswax candle smoke.

"There it is," she said. The towering pipe organ was built into the side of the chancel. At this hour its oak paneling was dappled red and blue with sunlight passing through stained-glass windows on the west side of the church. Every time she came into St. Bede's, it was slightly different—the light of morning, the light of afternoon, the darkness—and every time she had to catch her breath at the strange beauty of the place; it was like seeing the face of a loved person.

He went straight to the keyboard, pausing only for an almost imperceptible bow to the high altar, and sat himself down on the old oak bench. *Looks like he knows what he's doing*, she thought, as he flicked on the switch without even having to search for it. With a soft hiss the organ warmed up, and Mac Barrow began to play.

Even without all the keys sounding, it was—

there was no other word for it—heavenly. Mother Grey was fond of Bach. How did he know? The very church seemed to shudder with delight.

"Needs new leathers," he said matter-of-factly, shutting off the switch. "I think I can get the necessary materials this week. Can you let me have a key?"

"You play beautifully," she said. "Let me run it past my senior warden." This was what she always said when she wanted to think something over. Ralph Voercker was her senior warden; he was in Illinois this week driving a truck for his uncle's company and could not be reached. When he did come back, anything Mother Grey wanted to do would be fine with him. But Mac Barrow didn't have to know that. "Where can I get in touch with you?" she said.

He wrote his name, address, and phone number on a slip of paper and gave it to her. "If you like, we can meet for breakfast tomorrow at Delio's," he said. "I'll have some time before my first class. We can talk more about it then."

They stepped outside; she locked up the church. "Would you like a cup of coffee?" she said.

"I have to go," he said. "They're starting the hearing in five minutes. That's why I'm dressed like this." He held out the front of his jacket to display the COACH logo.

"What hearing?" Mother Grey hadn't read her *Clarion* this week.

"The town planning board is meeting to hear a proposal from some developer," he said. "If they accept, it'll mean the end of life in Fishersville as we know it."

"My word," she said. "But what is it that he wants to develop? We could use more low-income housing, you know. There are still homeless people here." From time to time Mother Grey had thought of trying to get herself appointed to the planning board. The task before the Fishersville planning board was both challenging and worthwhile. Over the last hundred years or so, poverty had kept the locals from tearing their old houses down or fixing them up according to their taste; these places, still authentically Victorian, were now eagerly sought after by people from outside with money. With the river on the west and the rocky cliffs on the east, there was nowhere to build new housing, and nowhere for the poor to live.

"We're not talking about a project for the homeless," Mac said. "This guy wants to put up another hotel for rich tourists."

"My word."

"But the thing is, he wants to build it on our Little League ball field."

"I get it. You coach for the Angels," she said, figuring out the significance of the jacket at last. "Do you mean Horace Burkhardt sold the ball field?" Surely Horace wouldn't sell the field out from under the poor little baseball players, would he?

"Evidently," he said. "I don't know the details of the land transaction. Yes, I'm one of the coaches for the Angels."

"Freddy Kane is on your team, and Garrett Hudson."

"Garrett's father is the Angels' head coach. Most

of the kids in town are involved in youth baseball, either tee-ball or Little League or girls' softball."

"It would be bad if they closed the field."

"I think so. You should come to the hearing, Mother Grey. The more people who show up, the more chance the planning board will turn it down."

"I think I will," she said. "I'll see you over there." If she was to make a public appearance on the side of truth and light, she must first wash her face and put on the clerical collar.

In Victorian times the Fishersville City Hall had been a big stone farmhouse; somewhere along the way the city fathers had attempted to convert it to the purposes of municipal government. The cramped cellar housed the city police department. On the first floor were the tax offices, where every year Mother Grey renewed the licenses for Towser and her little cat, Scratch. Also on the first floor was a courtroom–meeting room. There the city council met, the city boards held their hearings, and the municipal court held its regular sessions.

But that was inside. The gathering crowd had not yet been admitted when Mother Grey joined them to attend the planning board meeting. They were milling around on the lawn, on the sidewalk, all over the stone steps leading up to the locked oak doors. Mac Barrow was deep in conversation with another Angels coach, probably Tommy Hudson, and Officer Jack Kreevitch. Kreevitch was dressed in an Angels baseball hat and coach's jacket instead of his police uniform.

"Hi, Mother Vinnie." It was Freddy Kane, uniformed down to his cleats, accompanied by a similarly dressed Garrett Hudson. Coaches and children from other teams were there too, along with a park ranger in his Smokey the Bear outfit and several lawyers in gray business suits. What a photo-opportunity! But the media hadn't arrived yet.

Mother Grey smiled at Freddy and ruffled his hair; he was the only child there without a baseball cap. Then she spotted her friend Dr. Sheila Dresner, Towser's veterinarian.

"What are you doing here, Sheila?" Mother Grey asked.

"My dear, I'm defending my little home. Your friend Horace Burkhardt is trying to sell out to a consortium of greedy developers calling themselves Beetee Associates, so they can build a monstrosity on the Little League field."

"A hundred rooms. That's two hundred more tourists every weekend," Jack Kreevitch said.

"Beetee Associates?"

"Bunker Todd and his rich dentist backers."

"Ah. Bunker Todd," Mother Grey said. "The litigious developer of the *Clarion* stories." According to the weekly *Clarion*, Bunker Todd had seven or eight lawsuits pending at any given time against a number of governmental entities, mostly for business reasons, but sometimes it was personal. He sued the State of New Jersey to keep them from building the bike trail right next to his house. When he lost that suit he told the *Clarion* reporter that any workers who showed up and tried to build a bike trail beside his house would be shot.

They came to build the trail just the same. When Todd fell over some of their construction equipment and broke his leg, he again sued the state. Mother Grey remembered the story. LITIGIOUS DEVEL-OPER BREAKS LEG, the *Clarion* said.

"The man who's suing the state for pain and suf-fering," said Sheila. "That's the one."

"Yeah, really. Like it was the state that broke his leg," Kreevitch muttered.

"How did he break his leg, then?" Mother Grey asked him.

He didn't answer. The coaches were giving one another strange looks. Was there something mysteri-ous, embarrassing even, about Bunker Todd's bro-ken leg?

"Okay," she said, "then let me ask you this: How did this man get Horace to sell him the ball field?" Why would Horace Burkhardt, the same Horace Burkhardt who had given Mother Grey one of his own houses to live in rent-free when St. Bede's rec-tory burned down, sell the town ball field to an evil developer?

"Money," said Tommy Hudson, and he shot a look of intense hostility toward the doors of City Hall.

There at the top of the steps, waiting to go in before everyone else, was a solidly built man with a crutch, his right leg in a cast up to the middle of his thigh. He was standing on it with no particular show of pain and suffering; perhaps the cast served as a token of his intention to sue, to be left on until he received a settlement.

"My house is right next to this horrible thing they're planning to build. I'm very unhappy about it," Sheila said.

"I don't think anybody's for it," Tommy Hudson said.

"Jake is on the board, isn't he?" Mother Grey said.

"Yes," said Sheila, "but he can't vote on it because our property is too close. He has to abstain."

The doors opened; the crowd streamed into the courtroom. Mother Grey and Sheila found the last two seats. Many people packed into the back; some were left standing in the hall. Garrett and Freddy jumped up onto the broad windowsill, where they sat and played with a hand-held video game machine that went bleep, bloop, and played tinny music. From time to time over the general babble, Mother Grey could hear one of them cheering for himself: "Yesss."

Up in the front the planning board presided over the affairs of Fishersville from behind a judge's bench on a raised dais. The board chairman called the meeting to order and took roll. Two were absent. All the names were strange to Mother Grey except Jake Dresner and Rochelle Hudson. Rochelle wore a pinstripe business suit with big shoulders, thick makeup, and a great volume of hair, dyed champagne blond and carefully arranged for maximum impact.

"Is that Coach Hudson's wife?" Mother Grey whispered to Sheila.

"Right," Sheila said. Mother Grey and Sheila engaged in a running competition to see who could keep her finger most closely on the pulse of the town, although Mother Grey suspected that neither one of them really knew what went on here. Both were outcasts of a sort, an Episcopal priest in a town with few Episcopalians and a veterinarian in a town where few people had the resources to have their animals doctored. Still, they both tried to remember all the gossip they could.

"You know her from the school board," Mother Grey said. "She's the one you told me about who shouts when she doesn't get her way, right?"

"Right. She's also Jack Kreevitch's sister."

Score one for Sheila. "How did you know that?"

"Professionally," said Sheila. Having scored, she was entitled to hold out her hand and examine her nails in the ritual gesture. "Rochelle brought in Jack's dog once."

Mother Grey was about to ask what ailed Jack's dog when conversation was drowned in the increasing volume of growls from the people around them. Struggling to be heard over that and the noise of the air conditioner, the chairman asked people not to speak until the developer's presentation was over: "Members of the public will have ample opportunity . . . I must ask . . ." Rattle, buzz . . .

Mother Grey glanced around at the crowd, wondering who had come to speak in favor of the project and who against. In the front row the developer and his attorney fumbled with a number of large maps and charts. Just behind them sat the park ranger. Horace Burkhardt was nowhere to be seen.

The developer and his attorney gave their names as the board's attorney swore them in, Bunker Todd and Ben Hergemoller. Todd looked like ready money; the golf clothes, the solid flesh, the deep gleaming tan all seemed to speak of prosperous winters in sunny climes. Hergemoller smiled and made eye contact with the board members, a man easy and comfortable on his own turf.

"The lawyer's local, right?" Mother Grey said.

"Right," Sheila said.

Jake Dresner spoke up to remove himself from voting on the matter, since his house and garden were within two hundred feet of the proposed complex. "I do have certain things I would like to say as a private citizen," he said. "When Mr. Todd and counsel have finished, of course." Hergemoller shot him an uneasy glance.

"Since Mr. Dresner is abstaining and two members of the board are absent, Beetee Associates may want to postpone this hearing," the chairman offered. "As it is, the vote will have to be unanimous in order to pass a resolution."

"No," Hergemoller said. "We want to get on with it as quickly as possible."

So the project needed five votes to get past the board.

"Surely Rochelle Hudson will vote no," Mother Grey whispered. Rochelle Hudson was the wife of one of the Little League coaches. *Shouldn't she too remove herself from the voting?* Mother Grey thought. *Would they still have a quorum if she did?* But Rochelle kept mum. Curiously, Mother Grey thought she saw her exchange a look with the developer.

Then came the presentation. As everyone could see from the first big map displayed on the aluminum easel, the developer wanted to have his way with fifty acres along the river to put up a tourist hotel and convention center. THE RIVERSIDE HILTSHIRE, said the caption in fancy green lettering. The hotel was to have the third public elevator in the town, after the old folks' home and the library. It would feature an amphitheater, a heated Olympic-sized pool, a glassed-in upscale restaurant with a nice view of the wing dam, and a jet ski marina.

Soft hostile murmurings continued at the back of the room. But the real estate developer and his attorney seemed to be impervious to expressions of public scorn. With perfect serenity the two displayed their cardboard-mounted maps and architectural drawings and passed their photographs around the frowning semicircle of planning board members. Hergemoller made the presentation as though he had done it a thousand times before; his voice had such a soporific quality that Mother Grey nearly fell asleep where she sat.

The board questioned Todd and Hergemoller closely about parking. Would not the hotel draw burdensome numbers of cars into the already-overcrowded central business district? On an easel at the front of the room the presenters placed a multicolored site plan map. Beaming with confidence,

Ben Hergemoller pointed to the ample parking displayed there.

"What about floodplain restrictions?" asked one of the board members. No problem; they meant to build the place on pilings. The fifty-year flood mark, the hundred-year flood mark, all were carefully delineated on another map. Squinting, Mother Grey was able to discern a few Fishersville landmarks. Uneasily, she noted that the hundred-year mark lapped to the very steps of St. Bede's. Well, of course. Fishersville was a river town, after all. *The great flood of 'fifty-five. Was that the hundred-year flood or the fifty?* Maybe it was the fifty. In that case it would shortly be time for another. Perhaps she should begin looking for a cheap sump pump for the undercroft.

At last the developer's presentation was complete, and the public was invited to air their views.

Jake Dresner went first, voicing his unhappiness with the project as a near neighbor. He felt that an influx of tourists would bring down the value of his property. The project was a monster, he added, totally out of scale with the rest of the city. "In the afternoon its shadow will fall right across my wife's garden."

Jake was the only one there to speak solely as a homeowner. Nobody but the Dresners lived that far out in the south end of town; it was all light industry and public parks, except for Beetee's other project, a group of McMansions going up on the other side of the ball field, and no one had moved into them yet. Most of the citizen opposition to the Riverside Hiltshire came from the youth baseball league.

Mac Barrow spoke for them first. He stood up, a commanding presence. He said five miles was a long way to walk to a ball field. That's how far it was to the field in Weston. Right now the children could get to their field by themselves to play ball or to watch a game. This would end if the field were moved. Getting to games and practices would have to be much more structured, more organized. It would cut down the number of spectators, cut down the responsibility the kids themselves had for getting to practice and games, which was a big part, he said, of the character-building aspect of youth baseball. In short, it would be bad for the youth of the town. Grunts of assent came from the assembled townsfolk.

Young Garrett Hudson got down off the windowsill and gave a very dignified little speech about what youth baseball meant to him. He was planning on making a career in pitching, he said.

A slack-jawed young man in a muscle shirt, droopy shorts, and huge heavy shoes stood up and identified himself as a jet skier.

"State your name, please, sir," the chairman said.

"Randy Todd."

"That's Bunker Todd's son," Sheila whispered.

He was strongly in favor of the jet ski marina, he said. It would be a great asset to the youth of the town. Nearly everyone booed him. The chairman rapped for order.

"There's the mayor," whispered Mother Grey. Mayor Ron Budge leaned against the door jamb, keeping a neutral face. Clearly the Riverside Hilt-shire would bring in much-needed tax revenues, if it was successful. Equally clearly, Budge would call down the wrath of a significant number of voters upon himself if he said a word in its favor.

Two merchants spoke up for the new hotel; they liked it, they said, because it would attract trade.

"They're from out of town," Sheila muttered. A couple of the coaches hissed.

Coach Tommy Hudson stood up to say his piece. "I would like to point out that the tourist trade is irrelevant to the real life of the people of Fishersville, not like baseball, which as we all know is a true part of the American Dream." Cheers from the other coaches.

The chairman called on someone in the back row; it was Schwartz, one of Mother Grey's protégés from the halfway house for disturbed young men.

"I wish to speak in favor of this project," Schwartz said. His eyes were wild behind the thick glasses, his black hair uncombed, his chin dark with stubble. He spoke from notes on a card. "I think we can all agree that this is a free country. Our activities should remain free from government interference. The right of property, to develop our property as we wish, was granted to us in the Declaration of Independence." They thought he was finished, but he cleared his throat and continued. "As we know, baseball is a game that teaches children to submit to rules. This teaches the children to be fascists. As a libertarian, I am against rules of every kind. Thank you." He sat down.

Mother Grey made a note to speak to his therapist about increasing his medication.

George Pitts, the park ranger, rose to speak. Under his arm he had a large rolled paper that proved to be yet another map of the south end of town. The board's attorney swore him in. He put his map up next to the developer's display.

The ranger's map of the south end of Fishersville bore a streak of color that was absent from the developer's map, a corridor of red on either side of the canal. "This red strip is state land," the ranger said. "Public parkland. I call your attention to these thirty parking places on the map supplied by Beetee Associates."

"Let the record show that they overlap," muttered the board's lawyer. "Mark that exhibit twenty."

Public parkland. Naturally, he said, no one would be allowed to park cars there. He fixed the developer with the baleful glare he usually reserved for those who encouraged their dogs to frolic unleashed and defecate on the bike trail.

Drops of sweat popped out of attorney Hergemoller's pink brow.

"Of course we can alter the plan to the board's satisfaction," he said. "My client certainly would not wish to park cars on the state bike trail. Ha ha, that would be ridiculous. But while the new plan is being drawn up, I'm sure the board would have no problem approving—"

"We would definitely have to see the new plan," the chairman said, "before making any sort of ruling whatever." A second of silence while it sank in:

Beetee had lost the battle, without even taking a vote. The public broke into wild cheers. Boys high-fived each other. Team hats filled the air. The chairman rapped for order.

Hergemoller, still sputtering, insisted that to deny his client's desires would amount to an unlawful taking. They would be forced to seek an opinion from a higher court. But he could scarcely make himself heard above the jeering and the noise. The public surged out of the courtroom, the coaches pounding each other on the back.

3

The first thing Mother Grey did when she got back to the rectory was to call her friend Jane Bussey, who was on the staff of the Choir College.

"What?" she said, when Mother Grey had told her the purpose of the call. It was only ten-thirty; surely she hadn't gotten her out of bed. But alas, it seemed that she had.

"Mac Barrow," said Mother Grey. "He volunteered to play the old Hook and Hastings tracker organ at St. Bede's. Listen, if you're asleep, I can call you tomorrow."

"No, no, I had to get up anyway to answer the phone. What is it you want to know about him?"

"Is he reliable? Is he good?"

"He's reliable, he's good, he sings like an angel. He's also handsome, charming, elegant, well read, single, and as far as anyone here knows, he's straight. What, are you bothered because he's black?"

"Certainly not."

"Well, why are you calling me at this, you should excuse the expression, ungodly hour of the night?"

"He wants to work in my church. I'm calling you for a reference. So tell me. What's wrong with him?"

"Bad tendinitis in his right elbow. He can't do a whole lot of keyboard. But that shouldn't keep him from playing St. Bede's organ once or twice a week."

Still Mother Grey wasn't satisfied. "He doesn't . . . I don't know . . . sell drugs? Or murder young women?"

"Vinnie, why is it that you think every attractive man you meet is a serial killer?"

"He offered to work for me for free."

"Take him up on it. It's from God."

"Guess I will, then. Thanks."

"Good night," said Jane.

Mother Grey went to Delio's the following morning to meet St. Bede's new organist-choirmaster and to hand over to him the key to the church.

Mac Barrow hadn't yet arrived when she got there, but Horace Burkhardt was there having his breakfast all by himself. He was surrounded by the usual gang, but they were sitting at other tables with their backs to him. It was an odd scene.

"Morning, Mother Vinnie," Roscoe Hanks, the roofer, said to her as she came in. "Saw you at the planning board meeting last night." He spoke in a stagey voice, evidently for Horace's benefit.

"Good morning, Roscoe."

"Would you believe there would be anybody in town so low he would try to sell out the Little League ball field to a bunch of greedy developers?"

The others chimed in, taking advantage of the opportunity, if such it could be called, to snipe at the hated Horace.

"Used to be this was a nice place to raise kids."

"Used to be some people understood what life in a small town was good for."

"Some people grow up here and then forget. Their own grandchildren without a ball field."

"Shame."

"I'd hate to see the day I'd sink that far, is all I'm saying."

"Good morning, Horace," she said to the butt of all this malevolence, sitting at a tiny table with his coffee and cruller, seemingly six inches shorter than when she had seen him last.

"Morning, Mother Vinnie," said Horace. "You know, a man has a right to do what he wants with his own property. It's still a free country, least it was the last time I looked."

An inarticulate jeer issued from the other breakfasters, the only words of which Mother Grey could distinguish being "Yer ass, Horace." Mother Grey frowned at them.

"Sit down and have breakfast with me," Horace begged. Evidently she was the last person in town who was still talking to him.

"I can't," she said. "I'm meeting someone."

"*Et tu*, Mother Vinnie?" said Horace. "Everyone is against me. I guess I know when I'm not wanted. I guess a man can tell when he's lived too damned long."

It seemed that Horace was in need of pastoring. "Don't be silly, Horace," she said. "Bring your breakfast and sit at our table. There's only room for two where you are." He was not of her flock, of course, but attended the Roman church of St. Joseph the Worker. Nevertheless her duty was clear. He got up, cast his paper cup and plate peevishly into the trash, and hobbled out the door.

People were actually hissing. She thought of following after him, but then decided, no, Mac would be here in a minute, and she was in serious need of coffee. Later on she would call on Horace.

Coffee. She went to stand in line. As she was debating the merits of the various muffins, she heard a discreet throat-clearing behind her. Half expecting Horace again, she turned and looked into the blue eyes of Dave Dogg.

Not that long ago he had wanted to marry her. "Hi, Vinnie," he said shyly. "How are you?"

His voice still gave her a warm feeling. Funny how some perfectly ordinary-looking men could be wildly attractive simply by the beauty of their speaking voices. Or their hands. She loved well-shaped hands. Dave had a beautiful speaking voice and well-shaped hands, and she found him wildly attractive, even now. But it would have been a mistake for them to marry. She was almost certain. Her mission as vicar of St. Bede's consumed her whole life; what did she have left for a husband? And a cop at that. Cops were so needy, so terribly stressed. "I'm fine, Dave. What brings you to Fishersville?"

"Would you believe it, I'm here on a case," he said.

"Looking for murderers?"

"Tracking down murder weapons." They secured their breakfasts and sat down at the corner table. "There was a burglary here a few days ago where some guns were stolen. I don't know if you heard about it," he said.

"No."

"A guy named Todd over on North Canal Lane. Among other things, the burglars lifted his collection of constitutionally protected firearms."

"Not Bunker Todd?"

"You know him?"

"The most hated man in town. He wants to develop the kids' ball field into a resort hotel."

"Oh. Well, one of his guns was used last night in a convenience store robbery in Trenton. Sixteen-year-old night clerk shot dead. It's my case now."

"My word."

"I thought I'd go talk to this guy Todd, see if there's something the local police might have missed. So how's the world treating you? How are things at St. Bede's?"

"Getting better, Dave, little by little. I guess I have ten more families in the parish since the last time I talked to you."

"That's great, Vinnie. Great."

"Catch any good murderers lately?" she said.

"Every chance I get. So how are the Voerckers? Ralph staying out of trouble?"

"Saraleigh is working at the paper bag factory, and Ralph has a new job as a driver for his uncle's trucking company."

"No kidding. Ralph got a job?"

"It's a wonderful opportunity for him, but it keeps him on the road most of the time."

"Saraleigh is working too? What's she doing with the kids?"

"The girls go to Father Bingley's day care center, and now that school is out, Freddy spends the day at the halfway house. Danny Handleman is looking after him."

He frowned. "She leaves him with those nuts?"

"Freddy won't go to the day care center. He doesn't want to spend the summer with a bunch of babies, he said. So Saraleigh gets Danny to mind him and give him lunch while she goes to work, and in return she cleans up the house once a week for the boys. I guess it's a good arrangement. The Lord works in mysterious ways."

"Is he safe over there?"

"They aren't child molesters, Dave. Danny is obsessive-compulsive and Schwartz is a paranoid schizophrenic."

"Oh. Okay."

"Really, Danny takes good care of Freddy. He feeds him breakfast and lunch every day. And you should see how clean he keeps his face and hands."

"Right."

"I'm monitoring the situation."

"It's none of my business, anyway, Vinnie."

He sipped his coffee. She played with her stirrer. Then they both spoke at once and stopped. She tried again. "Are you and Felicia—" She couldn't quite figure out how to phrase it politely: remarried? sleeping together? dating? Are you sweeties again?

"I'm back with Felicia," he said. "We haven't made it legal yet."

"Ah."

"Felicia is serious about AA this time, and I thought it would be good to spend time with Ricky. Before he gets too old. But you know what? He doesn't talk to us. He just grunts. And he stays in his room."

"Listening to music?"

"Not even that. Kids don't like music anymore, not the way we used to do. No, he plays these video games, or thinks, or plots mass murders, I dunno. Teenagers. So what about you, Vinnie? Have you—"

"I have replaced the Weaver," she said. "Some money turned up last year."

"You bought a new cello?"

"Yes."

"Oh. That's great," he said.

"I have three students now, including little Freddy. And then Sheila Dresner and I get together to play once a week, along with two other musicians, so we can do quartets. But even better than that, I seem to have an organist for St. Bede's."

"That's really great."

"By the grace of God, a keyboard musician has

presented himself and offered to work for nothing. Matter of fact, I'm meeting him here this morning."

Dave's face was really strange as she unfolded these pieces of news, going through changes. He looked as if he were expecting something else. Maybe that she would have found another man by now, with him out of her life.

Just then Mac Barrow arrived. He stood for a moment framed in the doorway, impressively handsome. She waved. Dave looked him up and down as he put in his breakfast order and picked up his coffee. She introduced them when he came over and sat down.

"Dave Dogg, Mac Barrow," said Mother Grey. Dave's face was still a study; he seemed oddly uncomfortable. Then suddenly his jaw dropped. "Not *the* Mac Barrow?"

"Yes, I suppose so," Mac said.

"I have followed your career with great interest," Dave said.

"No kidding. You're a Phillies fan?"

"Sure. Everybody around here is either a Phillies fan or a Yankees fan. I can't root for the Yankees." He finished his coffee. "I saw you pitch that game against the Astros three years ago. You were fantastic. You never should have quit."

"I hurt my arm. Between that and the strike, I just didn't want to do big-league ball anymore. Not even the money was worth it." He put his coffee down, spread his hands. "I wanted to do what I wanted to do."

"Play a church organ?"

"Sure. And sing, and teach music." He grinned at Mother Grey, fellow musician, as if to say, *We understand, he doesn't.*

And he didn't. "What a waste," said Dave.

"Hey, listen, I coach a Little League team," said Mac. "I'm helping to keep the dream alive."

"I'm coaching a team too," Dave said. He seemed to feel this was not a reason to claim significance as a human being, like big-league pitching. "If I could pitch like you, I wouldn't stop until they made me stop."

Mac shrugged. "I can't pitch like me anymore either, Dave. It's not the end of the world. There is a life after baseball."

Dave looked back and forth from Mac Barrow to Mother Grey. "Good luck to you, man," he said finally. He got up and shook Mac Barrow by the hand. "Nice talking to you. I gotta go." He collected his paper plate and cup. "See you, Vinnie."

" 'Bye, Dave." Routed, she wasn't sure how, the intrepid detective went out to fight crime.

"So that's Dave Dogg."

"Yep," she said. Where had he heard about Dave Dogg? Jack Kreevitch must have been gossiping.

"I thought he would be taller than that," Mac said as Rose brought him his eggs.

"He's tall enough," she said. "Let's talk about what you want to do at St. Bede's."

He smiled. "Okay." Out of his rucksack came a folder of organ music. They talked about forming a choir, about hymns and anthems, not mentioning Dave again.

* * *

At the halfway house Freddy checked in, looking for breakfast. He did not have his new gun with him. He had left it in the cello case at home, since that was where the threat would come and where he must prepare his defenses.

He closed the back door carefully to keep the flies out, the way Danny always told him. Danny and Schwartz looked up from the table. Hot oatmeal and stewed prunes in the middle of June—Danny's idea of health food. Must be his turn to cook today.

Schwartz's whiskers were starting to get long, black, and fuzzy against his white skin. "Are you letting your beard grow again?" Freddy asked him.

Schwartz narrowed his eyes behind the thick glasses. "That's my business."

"Where's Frank?"

Both men sighed. Danny put the paper down. "Frank had another episode last night," he said. "He's back in the medical center."

"What's an episode?"

"Trust me, kid, you don't want to know," said Schwartz. "Life with a bunch of nuts is no picnic, let me tell you."

"Get some breakfast now, Freddy," Danny said. "Wash your hands first. Use the germicidal soap."

"Okay." Danny was supposed to be officially in charge of Freddy. Mother Grey had arranged this, as part of the social work she did, after Freddy refused to go to the stupid baby day care center with his little sisters.

But it was Schwartz that Freddy liked to hang out with, Schwartz who liked weapons and soldiers the way Freddy did, Schwartz who had been such a big help the time they tried to kill Freddy's ex-stepfather. All Danny had done the whole time that was happening was stand around and find fault.

Also Schwartz didn't give people a hard time about how often they washed their hands or whether the iron might still be plugged in or the water left running in the upstairs bathroom. And his computer had cool games, for which he knew all the cheat codes. He was the first person in Fishersville who found out how to get into god mode on Wolfenstein, and when he did, he let Freddy kill Hitler. Schwartz was almost like a regular kid.

For example.

"I dreamed about a gun last night," Schwartz said. Freddy couldn't tell which one of them he was talking to. Maybe he was talking to himself. Or maybe he was trying to annoy Danny; if so, it worked.

"What of it?" Danny said. "You always dream about guns. You have problems with aggression and paranoia, Schwartz. That's one of the reasons why you're living here."

"At least I don't wash my hands seven hundred and fifty times a day."

The oatmeal was cold and gummy, but if you mixed it with the prunes, it wasn't too bad. "What kind of gun did you dream about?" Freddy asked.

"An AK-47. I was holding it in my hand. It was very real, like holding a woman."

"Why would you want to hold a woman?"

"No reason. I tell you, though, I would really like to own a firearm."

Danny folded up his newspaper. He came over and put his face in Schwartz's face. "You can't have a gun," he said, speaking slowly and clearly. "You're certifiably insane."

"If the people around me would stop telling me that, I could get better a lot faster."

"Not with guns, you won't. Forget it, Schwartz." Danny picked up his coffee. "I hate it when he gets like this," he said, and went out of the kitchen.

Schwartz is right, Freddy thought. It was good to have a gun. But maybe it wasn't enough.

Maybe what he really needed to do was look for his real father.

This man was somewhere in Fishersville, or so he had gathered from hints dropped by his mother. If only he knew who he was, Freddy could ask him for help getting rid of Rex.

"Schwartz, can I ask you something?"

"Fire away."

"Do you know who my real father is?"

For the first time that morning, Schwartz looked straight at Freddy. "What makes you ask?"

"My mom won't tell me who my father is." He took his spoon and drew a face in the oatmeal. "Is it you?"

Schwartz ran his fingers through his hair. It stuck straight up, black and greasy. "Son," he said, "I have the greatest admiration for Saraleigh, but we have never been intimate in that way."

"What?"

Schwartz frowned and pulled his lip. "You know where babies come from, right?"

"Fathers and mothers."

"Yes, but first the fathers and mothers have to . . ."

"Oh, right, that. Yeah, I know all about that."

"Your mother and I never did that, Fred. If I have children I don't know about, you aren't one of them. It was some other guy."

"Oh."

"Isn't Ralph a good father to you?"

"He's never home anymore. Ever since his uncle gave him a job, he's away in the West all the time driving a truck."

"Well, what is it you need from him? Maybe I can help, even if I'm not your real father. I can be, like, your uncle."

"It's Rex."

"Rex Perskie. I see."

"I'm scared he's back. He calls on the phone and stuff, and now I'm having these nightmares."

"Has he come around to the apartment?"

"Sort of. I think I saw him through the window."

"This is going to be a problem," Schwartz said. "If Rex is really back. We have seen that he can't be killed by hitting him on the head."

"Maybe you could use a knife," Freddy suggested. "If you cut him in pieces and sent the pieces to different cities."

Schwartz shook his head. "I'm not that crazy. They put people who do things like that in padded cells, son, and then they lock the door and throw away the key."

"What if I got you a gun? Would you shoot him?" *Maybe I could lend Schwartz my gun until he kills Rex for me.* Actually, Schwartz could have the gun for keeps after that, since Freddy wouldn't need it anymore. But what if Rex came and got them all while Schwartz had Freddy's gun? He would have to get him some other gun then.

A slow smile spread across Schwartz's face. "Oh, yes. Get me a gun, and I'll shoot anybody you like."

4

At their cello lesson later that day, Mother Grey asked Freddy how he had liked the planning board meeting. She was interested in his reaction to what was probably his first experience of city government, always an important education in civics for the young.

"Cool," he said.

"Cool?"

"I mean, that was great, the way the ranger fixed those guys," he said. "Wasn't that great? They can't take away our ball field, right?"

"I hope not. It looks as though the planning board won't let them. You like baseball, don't you?"

"It's my sport," he said simply, the way he might have said, "It's my life."

"I've never seen you play."

"You should come to a game," he said. "We have one today. The Angels are versing the Rockies at six o'clock. It's at the Little League field."

"Okay, I will."

He seemed preoccupied all through the lesson. Mother Grey began to suspect he had something on his mind. As he was packing his cello away, he revealed what it was, to her great surprise.

"Mother Vinnie, can I ask you something?"

"Certainly."

"Do you know who my real father is?"

Real father. "I thought it was Rex Perskie." But no, that's right, it wasn't.

"He's Britney's father. He used to be my stepfather before the fire. You remember the fire, right?"

"I remember it very well. You and I nearly died, because you went back to try to save my cello."

"Oh, yeah. I woke up in the hospital."

"What makes you wonder about your father, Freddy? Have you talked about this with Saraleigh?"

"She won't tell me who it is. I think it's somebody I know. I thought maybe you knew."

"I can talk to her about it if you want me to. But if I were you, I'd just be happy having Ralph for a father. He loves you very much."

"He's hardly ever home."

Should she meddle in this? Freddy dragged his cello case down the front steps of the rectory and headed homeward. She dialed Saraleigh's number, got a busy signal, and then suffered one of those moments of doubt that Dave used to encourage her to have so often: Was she poking her nose where it was not appropriate, in the guise of pastoring her sheep?

Finding Freddy's father for him. No, that wasn't

appropriate. Of course she herself could see what it was that he needed from a father, try to be a friend to him, and maybe have a talk with Ralph when he got back from the Midwest.

And talk to Saraleigh. Definitely.

The hour of the baseball game found Mother Grey parking her borrowed bike in the bushes and making her way toward the stands. The ball field was in a low swampy area by the river. To the north beyond the outfield could be seen the skeleton tops of a number of houses under construction, and she thought, *The developers are coming.* A lone turkey buzzard circled slowly, now over the development, now over the ball field. She turned her attention to finding a place to sit.

Saraleigh and her little girls were up in the bleachers sitting beside Marla Kreevitch. On the other side of Marla sat a wholesome-looking Rochelle Hudson, without the makeup and the shoulders. Marla and Rochelle, sisters-in-law. Small-town life. One of these days Mother Grey would have to make a chart. And that was just of the family relationships. She couldn't even begin to imagine the history of romantic entanglements among these people.

For example, who *was* little Freddy's father? When she could get Saraleigh alone, she would find a way to broach the subject tactfully. Because it was bothering Freddy. Saraleigh would want to know what was on her little boy's mind.

The women called to her: "Come sit with us, Mother Vinnie."

"Is this the Angels' cheering section?" she said, climbing up to park herself behind them.

"Wherever," said Saraleigh. "We all cheer."

Mother Grey's namesake, Baby Vinnie, sucked her thumb on Saraleigh's knee as her half-sister Britney ran up and down between the stands and the fence, playing tag with the younger Kreevitch children. Too bad Ralph was on the road all the time. It was wonderful that he had a job, of course, but he loved his family so much that it seemed a shame he couldn't be with them.

It was nearly game time. Freddy made a last-minute foray from the Angels' dugout to wheedle a dollar from Saraleigh. "For Big League Chew," he begged. She gave it to him, and he ran to the snack shack.

Mother Grey was mildly shocked. "You let him chew tobacco?"

"It's bubble gum," Saraleigh said. She drew a cigarette out of her purse and lit it. *I'm getting on her nerves again,* Mother Grey thought, and resolved not to comment on Saraleigh's child-rearing practices. But it was tough. She did nothing the way Mother Grey would have done it. For instance, here she sat smoking all over poor little Baby Vinnie, giving her respiratory problems and the Lord knew what.

And of course there was the problem of Freddy's father.

Not my business. "Gimme quarters," Britney said to Saraleigh. Her mother forked over, and Britney went toddling off to the shack with her little fat hands full of coins. When she came back, she was sucking on a frozen blue and red thing in a paper cone, her pretty face grotesquely stained with food coloring. Revolting. And that was only what it did to her outsides. *Keep quiet about it*. Mother Grey bit her lips.

Was there anything fit to eat in the shack? Feeling hungry, Mother Grey went to check it out. She stood in line behind the children and read the hand-lettered list of treats for sale. The hot dogs and frozen pizza seemed acceptable, but it was too early. Everything else was made of sugar and chemicals.

Except for the Philadelphia-style soft pretzels. "I'll have a pretzel," she said to the woman in the window, as the child in front of her slathered his steaming pretzel with yellow mustard. The smell was tempting.

"I just sold the last one. Next batch will be ready in another seven or eight minutes, if you want to wait." As Mother Grey watched, the woman took a few out of the freezer, moistened them, dipped them in kosher salt, and put them in the toaster oven.

"I'll come back," said Mother Grey. There was some sort of theological lesson to be learned here; you could get candy right away, but you had to wait for pretzels. With further thought she might be able to work it into Sunday's sermon. She went back to the bleachers and sat down again.

From the Angels' dugout came the voice of coach Tommy Hudson pouring spirit into his team. Mother Grey could not understand what he was shouting, but the form was call-and-response; the coach would holler something, and the children would bark a reply. When they were sufficiently fired up, they all came running out onto the field cheering, or maybe growling in high voices, to take their places around the diamond. They threw baseballs at one another with great energy, catching them maybe half the time.

"There's Freddy," Saraleigh said. The child who tottered out of the dugout was almost buried under catcher regalia. Mother Grey would never have recognized him. Garrett Hudson began throwing him practice pitches.

Recent rains had made the outfield grass grow enormously lush and green, high as the tops of the players' baseball shoes. Gnats rose up out of the grass to form clouds around the heads of players, coaches, and spectators. The odor of Avon's Skin-So-Soft hung on the steamy air. Rochelle Hudson tugged at her Angels hat, which had some kind of pink tissue stuck in it.

"What's that in your hat?" Saraleigh asked her.

"Dryer sheet," Rochelle said. "Keeps the gnats away." Sure enough, a number of the women in the stands had tucked tissues of smelly fabric softener into their headgear.

Mother Grey admired these adornments. "Maybe I should try that," she said. Gnats were flying up her nose. It was true that she didn't keep dryer sheets in the house; she hadn't any dryer but hung her clothes out to dry on a line. Her stomach rumbled, and she thought, *Four more minutes.*

Then it was time to get serious; all the balls were thrown in except the one in the hands of the pitcher. The outfielders assumed a half-crouch, hands on knees, that indicated their readiness to play. Over the public address system a child's voice announced the Rockies' batting order. The first of the Rockies stepped up to the plate. As the Rockies' mothers shouted words of encouragement ("You can do it, Chuckie! Hit it over the fence!"), he waggled the bat in a spirited fashion and shifted his weight from one foot to the other.

Garrett pitched a fast one, and Chuckie fanned it.

Dave Dogg appeared at the back of the stands and climbed up beside Mother Grey.

"What are you doing here?" she said.

"I thought I'd like to watch an Angels game," he said. He took out a pair of field glasses and looked the players over.

"Let's talk it up out there," called Coach Hudson, and the outfielders began to bleat like sheep, "Ga-a-arrett, Ga-a-arrett." Thus encouraged, Garrett wound up and pitched another fast ball. "Strike!" bellowed the umpire.

Jack Kreevitch had taken up the position of third-base coach, standing near the high chain-link fence. He glanced over and saw Dave Dogg. "Yo, Dave," he called. "You scouting for the Trenton Thunder?"

"Sure," Dave said, getting down from the bleacher seat. "Are all your little guys wearing their hats today?"

"Of course. Our little guys always wear their hats."

"Is that so. I'm glad to hear it," Dave said, and he approached the fence, continuing to speak to Kreevitch, though in such a low voice that Mother Grey was unable to hear what he said. Kreevitch stood listening with his hands in his back pockets, blowing a huge purple bubble. Even the coaches used Big League Chew. It occurred to her that Dave had not come here to see her, that in fact he was here in his professional capacity. It annoyed her to realize that she was disappointed.

As Dave went around behind the fence and disappeared into the Angels' dugout, Mother Grey became aware of the murmur of conversation behind her. With horror she heard the women openly admiring the rear ends of the coaches. Of all things. She could just imagine what her grandmother would have said about such talk. Very ordinary, Granny would have said, by which she would have meant vulgar, since well-bred people never came right out and called other people vulgar, any more than they made public remarks about each other's bottoms. But, you know, the coaches did wear their pants kind of tight, and Saraleigh was perfectly right; Mac Barrow had nice buns.

The pretzels were ready. She went and got hers, added mustard, and returned to the stands in time to overhear the end of a discussion of what to do when you win the lottery. About that time the Rockies made their third out.

Rochelle Hudson seemed to have her plans all

set for her lottery winnings: hot cars, fancy clothes, trips to the islands, skin-diving, skiing.

"Has Tommy found another job yet?" Marla asked her.

"Not yet. They offered him something in Texas, but he doesn't want to leave Fishersville. And of course my business is here."

"How's that doing?"

"Real estate is not booming the way people seem to think."

"So what would you do, Vinnie, if you won the lottery?" asked Marla.

"If I played the lottery, and I won the lottery, I guess I'd spend it on paint for the church," she said. Long ago Mother Grey had turned her back on material wealth (presuming she ever could have had a shot at it) in favor of spiritual riches. Although now that she thought of it, the last time she had come into unexpected money, she had spent it on cellos, one for Freddy and one for herself, and on an expensive New York City hairdo so artlessly simple that no one in town had noticed it. So. She was exposed in her own eyes as a hypocrite.

Saraleigh exhibited no shame about wanting big money. "Maybe Ralphie will make some, working for the trucking company. Maybe his uncle will drop dead and leave it all to him."

"After a long and fruitful life," Mother Grey amended.

"Oh, yeah. Yeah. A long and fruitful life. The fruitfuller the better."

Rochelle was not inclined to agree about the desirability of waiting for pie in the sky. "I'm sick of being poor," she said.

"Weren't you handling the transaction between Horace and Beetee Associates?"

"Yeah, and we see how that's shaping up, don't we? Plus the fact that I'm not pleased with life at my house right now," she said. "Now that my Dawn is fourteen, she thinks she's queen of the universe. Ever since she quit softball, she's not my little girl anymore. Nothing I do is right."

"She quit softball?" Marla was aghast. "I knew she stopped baby-sitting, but quit softball! She was so good at it."

"Quit softball, started smoking cigarettes, and God knows what. Too good for softball. Too good to work. Queen of the universe. Her grades are in the toilet. Tommy says he's going to have to get her a shopping bag and find her a grate when she gets out of school. And rude! I wouldn't even want to tell you some of the things—" Then Garrett came up to bat, and she switched her attention to cheering him on in a loud voice.

Five fourteen-year-old girls with the frisky look of young ponies approached the bleachers. They walked almost in step, holding themselves beautifully erect, aware that they might be looked at. They had painted their faces, dark lipstick, dark eyeliner. One wore hennaed hair. As they climbed up beside Mother Grey, searching for seats, the hennaed one leaned over and said to Rochelle, "Mom, I'm going to the mall."

"What mall? The nearest mall is twenty miles away."

"My girlfriends and I are going to the mall. Dad said it's okay. Can I have some money?"

"What is that on your hair, young lady?" Rochelle said.

"We're going to the mall. Okay? So give me some money."

"What mall? You didn't do your chores."

"What chores?"

"I'll give you till the count of three to go home and wash that paint off."

"Mom."

"Get going. One . . ."

"Mom!!!"

"Two . . ."

"You never let me do anything! You *bitch*! You get to run around with that fat developer behind dad's back, and I can't even put a rinse on my hair! I *hate* you! I wish you were *dead*!!"

Smack! The blow passed so close to Mother Grey's face that it nearly got her. Dawn shrieked. Rochelle, through gritted teeth, said, "Right home, young lady." She grabbed her daughter by some part of her scanty clothing, and as the others pretended not to notice, she dragged her away.

The girls who had come with her got down out of the bleachers, some slumping their shoulders, some ducking their heads, some rolling their eyes, and went away in the opposite direction.

"Fat developer?" Saraleigh murmured.

"My word," said Mother Grey.

There was a long silence, and at last Saraleigh broke it with the scratch of a match as she lit another cigarette.

"It's not usually like this," said Marla. "Usually it's lots of fun in the stands. Everyone gets along."

"You should come to the next game," said Saraleigh. "Then you can get more of an idea."

They all stared at the field. The child on the loudspeaker who announced all the plays from a tower over the shack reported that Fred Kane was up at bat.

Saraleigh cheered lustily.

Mother Grey found herself shouting too: "All right, Freddy!"

The Rockies outfielders bleated at their little pitcher, "Ma-a-att, Ma-a-att."

Matt wound up, the ball left his fingers, and there was a tremendous clong! as the aluminum bat whacked the ball smartly.

A hook? A slice? Anyway, the ball went straight into the outstretched glove of the first baseperson, a tall young girl with high-topped cleats. Freddy halted in his mad dash to first and returned crestfallen to the dugout, dropping his protective hat in the pile of hard hats by the fence.

"Kane grounds out to first," came the laconic announcement.

But things picked up later, as Fred's teammates made a few base hits.

By the second half of the third inning, the score was five to three. Freddy and Garrett Hudson came around collecting money for the youth baseball association. They held out their Angels hats while each spectator dropped in a dollar.

"Where's my mom?" said Garrett.

"She and your sister had to go home," Marla said.

As she put in her offering, Mother Grey noticed Ralph's name written in Freddy's hat.

Saraleigh noticed it too. "Better be careful of that hat," she said. "It belongs to your dad. What happened to your hat?"

He felt his head, almost as if he expected to find it there. "I dunno," he said.

5

The following day was sparkle day. Once a year the mayor and city council of Fishersville declare a day when everyone may put discarded possessions out on the street, to be carried away regardless of the usual regulations. Refrigerators, upholstered furniture, building trash, and suchlike are not normally accepted by the city trash haulers except on sparkle day. The date is kept secret from the citizens of other towns lest they bring their own garbage and dump it on Fishersville's streets. No mention is made even in the *Clarion*, but one sole announcement goes out with the trash and recycling pickup schedule distributed with the tax bills at the beginning of the year, only to property owners.

Mother Grey knew about it, of course. Sheila Dresner would score a good fifteen points in the ear-to-the-ground competition if Mother Grey ever let an event like sparkle day get past her. At seven in the morning she began hauling to the curb the many

Items Checked Out Today:
Title: Cavendon Hall
Author: Bradford, Barbara Taylor
Barcode: 20104555
Due: 10/7/2015

Title: The Cavendon women
Author: Bradford, Barbara Taylor
Barcode: 20106263
Due: 10/7/2015

Title: The Winter People
Author: McMahon, Jennifer
Barcode: 7251306597
Due: 10/7/2015

Title: The naked eye : [a novel]
Author: Johansen, Iris
Barcode: 20106748
Due: 10/7/2015

Title: Badlands
Author: Box, C. J.
Barcode: 20106806
Due: 10/7/2015

sparkle things of St. Bede's: five half-dead vacuum cleaners, two twenty-year-old refrigerators, nine cubic yards of unwanted books, all gifts to the church from a generous citizenry. On any other trash day the city would charge the church to carry these things away.

Horace Burkhardt emerged from his house next door, wrestling an old mattress out to the curb.

"Good morning, Horace," she said. "How are you? I've been meaning to call you."

He grunted, dropped the mattress, and went back for the box spring. There was a pile in front of his house already. Unusual. People his age who were inclined to throw things out had normally thrown it all out years ago.

"I'm terrible," Horace said, putting the box spring down on the curb. "My daughter's out of town, nobody will talk to me except you, and now my girlfriend wrote and broke up with me." He pulled a many-folded letter out of his shirt pocket. "I got her letter yesterday. Look at this."

Handwritten on yellow paper with flowers in the upper corner, it was a sort of Dear John letter from somebody in St. Augustine who signed herself Honey. Mother Grey had to read it over twice to make out her handwriting in places. Honey was writing to say that she had heard from her son Jack what Horace planned to do with the ball field, kicking her grandchildren out of their source of recreation, health, and sport. She found it impossible to forgive him, she said. He was not the man she thought he was. They must rethink their wedding plans. *Jack? Not . . .*

"I had no idea you were planning to be married," she said. "But if she's right for you, surely—"

"Thing is, it was for her I was selling, so we could have some money. Now it's all for nothing."

"Tell me about this lady. Where did you meet her?"

"Right here in Fishersville."

"Was she your old high school sweetheart?"

"No, she was in kindergarten when I was going to high school. But I used to know her when my wife was alive, and her husband too. Matter of fact, she worked in my real estate office, oh, it must have been thirty years ago. She still has kids in town. You know Jack Kreevitch, don't you?"

"You're engaged to Jack's mother." She made another mental note for her relationship chart.

"Was engaged, looks like." He folded up the letter and with a sigh put it in his back pocket. "I've been going to Florida every winter ever since I retired. I knew Honey had a condo in St. Augustine, and I just started looking her up whenever I was there. She didn't seem to mind."

"So romance blossomed," said Mother Grey.

"Yep. Year before last, when the weather was so bad and I was stuck here all winter, sick most of the time, all I could think of was going south to be with Honey, staying down there where it was warm, never coming back. So last winter I went back to St. Augustine, and she said she would have me. I only came back here to wind up my affairs, sell off my property and all. We were planning a nice quiet wedding in Florida, no children, no grandchildren, no dogs, no cats, just us." He took out the letter again and replaced it in the pocket over his heart. "What a mess."

"But you haven't closed the deal for the field with Bunker Todd, have you?"

"No, but he won't let me out of it. He says we have an ironclad contract. Not in your hands anymore, I'm afraid, he says to me. He and his lawyer both, the bloodsucking—"

"Maybe they won't be interested anymore after what the planning board decided."

"No, they say they'll appeal, they're going to ram it through if it takes twenty years. I'm stuck with it. I'm dead."

"You ought to see your own lawyer."

"Did that. He says the same. Now my girl has quit me. Seduced and abandoned, is what I am. Lived too damned long. Your church approves of euthanasia, right? You'll let them bury me out of St. Bede's, won't you, Mother Grey, after I kill myself."

"I'm sure it won't come to that, Horace," she said. But was she? Or was it time to dust off her pastoring-of-the-suicidal skills? "You know, if you really feel you might harm yourself, I want you to come and see me first. It may help you to talk about it." Also she could call ahead to the County Medical Center's mental ward, reserve him a bed, and give him a ride over there. This was a drill she knew well from the days before Ralph had found happiness with Saraleigh.

"That's all right," he said. "I'm fine." They went back in their houses. Seven-fourteen; if Mother Grey called right away, she could still catch Saraleigh before she left to take her little girls to the day care center. So many lives to meddle in, so little time.

When she dialed the Voerckers' number, the regular ringing sounded, and not the usual bee-bee-*BEEP!* followed by the annoying message that this number had been disconnected. They must have paid their phone bill on time this month. So Ralph's new job was working out nicely, on an economic level at least.

Saraleigh picked up after the third ring. *Try to be tactful.* After the usual greetings Mother Grey said, "Saraleigh, I'm calling about Freddy. I think he's having problems."

"What kind of problems?"

"He asked me yesterday to help him find out who his real father was. Is something bothering him?"

Saraleigh sighed. "I dunno. Last night he insisted on sleeping in my bed and bringing his cello case with him. He says someone is after him, or someone is following him. Can you beat that? Kids."

"Who is his father?"

A chilly silence, then, "That's my business, Mother Vinnie."

"Did he desert you? Was he married?" *Tactfully, now, Vinnie.*

"I don't want to talk about it." Rustle, scritch, puff, Saraleigh was lighting up a cigarette. "When my parents kicked me out, I wouldn't even tell the

62

County Welfare Board who he was. That was eleven years ago, and nobody cares anymore."

"Freddy seems to be . . . he seems concerned."

"Ralph is his father." Of course that couldn't be true, biologically speaking. Saraleigh and Ralph hadn't even met until the week before the rectory fire.

"Well, what do you think? Do you think he's being followed? Do you think someone's bothering him?"

"No, I don't. He made it up. Why would anyone follow Freddy? I'll talk to you later, Mother Vinnie. I have to go to work now."

The Reeker brothers were also up early. It was always good at any hour to get out of the house and away from their surly mother and pesky little brothers, but now they had someplace to go, and something exciting to do when they got there.

They were using their guns for target practice. Nobody ever heard the shots when they did this. You wouldn't think gunshots would go unnoticed in a quiet town the size of Fishersville, but with the Fourth of July approaching, odd bangs and pops formed a part of the background ambience along with the rescue squad sirens and the fire horn. Some parts of town were noisier than others; one of these was the gravel quarry on the north side. The quarry's grinding chugging roar, the sound of an entire mountain being reduced to crumbs, masked the sound of gunfire quite successfully.

Garrett Hudson knew where his friends were meeting that day for gun fun. He found the Reeker boys blazing away at soda cans behind the ledge at the top of the quarry.

Howie was the first to greet him. "Hi, Garrett. Hey, I saw your sister in the bank parking lot this morning. She was with that guy again."

"Uh-huh." The last thing Garrett wanted to talk about was his stupid sister.

"She had her tongue in his mouth," Howie said.

"Sick," said Chick.

"Let me borrow your gun," Garrett said to Chick. "I want a shot."

"Where's yours?"

"I dunno."

"Where'd you leave it?" said Howie.

"In my underwear drawer."

"Brilliant. Your mom got it, I bet."

"She never looks there. I put away my own laundry."

"Who took it then?"

"I dunno. It was there one day, and the next it was gone."

"I bet your sister took it," said Howie.

"Why would my stupid sister want a gun?"

"Ask her. Anyway you're not getting mine."

"Here," said Chick. "Just one shot, though. See if you can hit that can."

"With just one shot?"

"Sure. You could do it. I did."

He took the pistol and held it out with two hands, like the cops on television, though it was smaller than the TV guns. It wasn't a revolver like the gun he had lost but the kind that took a clip. He could feel bumps on the cold metal of the grip. On the end of the barrel was a sight. He lined it up through the notch to point at one of the soda cans and slowly squeezed the trigger the way he always heard you were supposed to.

Blam. The gun had a kick, not just backward but to the left, when the cartridge popped out of the right side of the gun. That must have been what made him miss the soda can, the kick. He knew he could shoot better than that. One more shot. He'd take one more before Chick could get the gun back.

Blam, whine. The shot missed the soda can again, but this time it ricocheted and came back at them. Howie screamed and put his hand up to his head. When he held it out, it was bloody.

Half a mile from the quarry, Dave Dogg and Jack Kreevitch were touring the town by bicycle. Dave had borrowed a mountain bike from the Fishersville police.

Kreevitch was guiding him to all the hidden corners of the town that were not accessible by car. So far they had traversed the back alleys, cruised up and down the canal bike path, followed the railroad tracks to where the hobby-railroaders parked their spare railroad cars, and checked out the environs of the wing dam. All these places showed evidence of kid gang activity: graffiti, empty beer bottles, rags, the ashes of old fires. When they found empty shells,

Dave collected and tagged them in a plastic evidence bag. Nowhere had they seen any actual kids.

They both thought the gun burglary to be the work of locals. But which ones? Kreevitch couldn't tell; he no longer knew everyone in town, not even all the bad boys.

Maybe one of the Angels was involved, maybe not. While it was true that all the boys wore baseball hats these days, whether they were on a team or not, the original Angels, the big league ball team, were based on the West Coast, such a long way from New Jersey that you just didn't see a lot of Angels hats in town. Fishersville was hardly a hotbed of Angels fans. On the other hand, the hat could have been planted.

"So how long have you guys been using bicycles to patrol the town?"

"Six months," Kreevitch said. "I lost ten pounds." He was in great shape. Dave thought, *I should get a bicycle, pedal around Ewing Township*. It was not the sort of activity homicide detectives usually engaged in, but what the hell, maybe it would do him some good. He and Ricky could get out of the house on the weekends, go riding. Get on the canal path, pedal ten miles to Fishersville. Felicia could even come along. His daydream reached the point where they all went to Delio's for ice cream and ran into Vinnie—Felicia and Vinnie face to face at last—and he thought, okay, maybe not, maybe he would just join a health club.

Kreevitch veered off the road onto a well-worn dirt trail. Up through the woods they climbed. Kreevitch wasn't even short of breath. Not like Dave. Maybe it was the gears. If only Dave could work the gears right, he could charge up these hills without breaking a sweat.

They had almost reached the top of the hill by the stone quarry when they heard a couple of bangs over the roar of the quarry's machinery.

"Gunshots," Kreevitch said. They began to pedal like madmen.

When they topped the rise, they could see down into a little grotto surrounded by scrubby trees. No one was in sight. Sunlight gleamed off a row of soda cans lined up against the rock wall below them.

The trail curved steeply around the rock wall. They dismounted and climbed down, carrying the bikes. Dirt and slippery leaves made bad footing; stones broke loose and rolled. More than once Dave thought he would fall or drop the bike. "You do this all the time?" he said when they reached the bottom.

"Keeps me fit," said Kreevitch, looking around.

They inspected the soda cans. One had a hole in it, right through the *o* in *Coke*. Good fingerprints. Into the evidence bag.

They found the cartridges fifty feet away. "Nice shooting," Dave said. Another evidence bag, another label.

Then they saw the blood. Had the little bastards hit an animal? Or each other? A line of red drops the size of nickels led to the entrance to another dirt trail.

Away off down the hill something moved or

flashed. Kreevitch said, "There they go," and he mounted his bike and went after them.

Dave Dogg followed, but he couldn't keep up; rocks and tree roots in the trail seemed almost to be rising up on purpose to dump him. At the bottom he found Kreevitch trying to raise the dispatcher on his radio.

The visible blood trail had petered out. "We need a dog," Dave said. Vinnie had a dog. He tried to picture Towser following a trail and decided the dog probably wouldn't want to fool with it. "Did you see which way they went?"

"All different ways," Kreevitch said.

"Maybe I could borrow a K-9 unit from Trenton," Dave said.

"We don't want your Trenton dogs in Fishersville," Kreevitch said. "Chewing up the taxpayers. This is a quiet community."

"For tracking," Dave said. "Not for biting people. Dogs have very sensitive noses." Quiet? The community was a hotbed of juvenile crime. Kreevitch must live in a dream world.

"Yeah, well, okay," said Kreevitch. "Do what you want."

While Kreevitch talked to his office, Dave used the cellular phone to get hold of his cohorts in Trenton and wheedle a K-9 unit out of them. Having done that, he hiked back up the hill to collect samples of blood, hoping it came from a rabbit or a squirrel. Kreevitch rode away to search for armed kids.

It was a good three-quarters of an hour before the K-9 officer from Trenton met them at the foot of the track up to the quarry. He brought a big German shepherd; he patted it and called it Ludwig. They went up to where the blood was. Ludwig seemed to understand what was expected of him, and he went straight to work.

Ludwig's demeanor was so professional that they all expected great things from him. After checking the blood drops, the dog led them very purposefully down the hill, across the street, and southward along the sidewalk, sniffing all the while. But when he stopped, it was on the front steps of St. Bede's rectory. He turned to the K-9 cop and barked once, as if to say, "Where's my doggie treat?" On the other side of the glass, Vinnie's little dog Towser, seeing another dog outside, went berserk.

Dave and Kreevitch stared at each other, then at Ludwig. Obviously this dog was retarded. Mother Grey would never harbor guns, gun-toting children, or violent persons of any sort under the roof of St. Bede's rectory. Dave feared that she would come to the door and catch them standing there, three policemen and an attack-trained German shepherd. She would have a few choice words to say. It wouldn't be pretty.

At last Kreevitch spoke. "See, that's the thing about dogs. All they're really interested in is other dogs."

The Trenton K-9 officer glared at them. "Aren't you even gonna knock?" he said.

"No," said Dave and Kreevitch together.

* * *

69

"Come on, Sparky. Here, boy." Horace was having difficulty getting his daughter's dog out of the public park and back on the leash. He had brought along the bag of doggie treats, and he shook them temptingly, but Horace had fed him so many of these in the past week in the effort to control him that the animal's appetite was becoming jaded. With Great Danes it was hard to exert a whole lot of physical control, not like with Horace's old beagle, which he used to hit with the newspaper and kick sometimes. He wouldn't like to try hitting Sparky.

"Come here, boy." Playfully the dog frisked behind a bush. He was still a puppy really, full of wild puppy spirits. Allison had no business going off and leaving him at such a young and uncontrollable age. Horace, furthermore, was no spring chicken, to be taking care of abandoned dogs while their abandoned women owners cavorted in Central American tourist resorts. Octogenarians should not be asked to chase puppies.

"Ahem."

There stood the park ranger, the dirty bureaucrat who had ruined the ball field deal and left Horace high and dry, the object of public scorn in Fishersville. He was gazing pointedly at Horace, his arms folded over his chest.

"I notice that your dog is moving his bowels on the bike trail," the ranger said.

Was that what he was doing? "Good," said Horace. "I was getting worried. He's been a little constipated since my daughter went to Mexico last week.

He's my daughter's dog, a purebred Great Dane. Did you ever see a bigger one?"

"Of course you always pick up after him, when he's finished doing his business," the ranger said. "It's a park rule, and there is also a city ordinance to that effect."

"What? Oh, sure."

"You brought something to pick it up with, didn't you?"

"Hanh?"

"Your animal's ordure."

"Not my animal. He belongs to my daughter. She's in Laredo. That's in Mexico, you know."

At this point Sparky came frisking back and sat at his feet, disposed once again to be cooperative. Horace reached for his collar to clip the dog's lead to it, but the dog backed up a few steps, grinning.

"I also notice that the dog is off his leash," the ranger said.

"Yeah. A big dog like that, he needs to run, right? Exercise. It's very important, my daughter told me."

"It's against park regulations." The ranger took out a pad. "The canal is a public waterway, the water is used for drinking by a number of communities, including this one. I'm going to have to write you a ticket, I'm afraid, sir. Could you tell me your name, please?"

"A ticket?"

"Sir, you have one minute to remove your dog and its droppings from this public park. If you do not, I'll have to find you in violation of NJAC 7:2–2.8(E) and write you a ticket."

"Most of the crap on this trail comes from your damned geese," said Horace. "I don't see you writing them any goddamned tickets."

"Sir, I must ask you not to raise your voice to me."

"Look at that, goose shit as far as the eye can see. You must be one of them goddamned environmentalists."

"Sir, I must insist that you pick up the dung from your animal and carry it away with you for disposal in a sanitary manner."

"I'll see you in hell first!!" People were passing by; they turned and stared. The dog still wouldn't come to him. Horace was mad enough to do murder.

6

The sun was climbing higher in the east as Mother Grey propelled her bike southward along the gravel trail, behind the Acme, past the sewage treatment plant, past the wing dam, toward the Fishersville flea market, about a mile beyond the Little League field. Since it was Wednesday, the market would be open, and since it wasn't Saturday, the crowds should be thin.

Her second-to-the-last dinner plate had broken the day before in one of those annoying accidents; a Dutch oven had fallen on it and smashed it in three pieces. She never should have left the pot teetering in the dish drainer but there was so much to do that the kitchen never seemed to get cleaned up properly, and now if she should have a dinner guest, there would be nothing to put his or her food on. Her plan was to find some cheap but attractive dishes at the flea market and carry them home in her backpack. Lots of free dishes lined the curbsides of Fishersville in boxes and bags for sparkle day, but they all seemed to be broken.

It was going to be a rough week for the priestly pocketbook. Not only must she replace the dish, she must also buy this bicycle, for twenty-five dollars plus the cost of some minor repairs, from her friend Sheila. In the week since she had taken up cycling, she felt more alert and energetic than she had in a long time. Two more weeks, and she might even find the starch to clean the kitchen.

Beyond the Little League field loomed the half-built houses, the tops of their roof-frames emerging from the shadow of the rocky cliffs to catch the sunlight. They were built along the lines of mansions, high, wide, pretentious, up on pilings because they were in the floodplain, each commanding an acre of stony subsoil and a view of the river. Four of the seven houses were in the process of having their roofs noisily applied. Men swarmed over them carrying materials, driving nails. Hammer blows echoed and reechoed in frantic counterpoint.

A new bridge, marked with the muddy tracks of construction traffic, crossed the canal from the housing development to the road. A sign read FISHERSVILLE HOLDINGS: HOMES BY BEETEE ASSOCIATES. Mother Grey had to detour around a dark green panel truck with the Beetee Associates logo on the door, parked right up next to the trail with its tail end hanging out. *The ranger will get you for that, Mr. Todd.*

She stopped to take a drink of water from the bottle so cleverly clipped to Sheila's bicycle, marveling at how modern life offered the most wonderful gadgets for sporting pastimes. She heard a murmur of voices and looked up. Braced against a nearby tree stood Bunker Todd himself, a cast on his leg, a hard hat on his head, a cigar in his teeth, his arms crossed over his chest, talking to someone.

Todd reminded her of a prize bull she had seen once at a livestock auction: the sleek skin, the fat-padded muscles. Close enough almost to smell him, she sensed exudations of testosterone. He was dressed as he had been at the planning board meeting, except for the hat, but he was not wearing his courtroom manners.

The man he was talking to stood in an attitude of dejection, half hidden from Mother Grey by a bush. Tattooed, denim-clad, the back of him looked familiar. With an unpleasant smile Todd spat vulgarities at him through the well-chewed cigar. Mother Grey was burning to know what they were discussing, but Todd noticed her interest as she wheeled her bicycle closer.

"What are you staring at, sweetheart? Like what you see?" And he made an obscene kissing face.

The man with him glanced at her. Rex Perskie! Saraleigh's old lover, the abusive Rex, was back in Fishersville! He murmured something to Todd, who said, "Oh. Well, shit, how was I supposed to know that? Who cares anyhow?" Without apology, he shifted his weight so that his back was to her and to the bike trail.

Clearly Rex had filled Todd in on her affiliation with the church. Once again the social curtain that separated her from the rest of sinful humanity came down. A good thing in Bunker Todd's case, if that was the way he spoke to strange women. As she passed, they continued to parley in low tones. Rex seemed to be whining.

Mother Grey rode away. So Rex was back. She offered a silent prayer for him to remain sober and to stay away from Saraleigh. She would have to call and warn her to keep the doors and windows locked.

More than a year had passed since Rex Perskie disappeared so mysteriously, after causing so much unpleasantness in the town. Hadn't Officer Jack Kreevitch been looking for him? Wasn't he, in fact, a wanted man? The thing to do would be to go straight to the police as soon as she got back to town and tattle on him.

7

A few hundred yards beyond Fishersville Holdings, another bridge crossed the canal to the main road. A muddy flat clearing opened out in the woods there. The cars of flea market customers were parked in the clearing and among the trees. Thick bushes grew all around. Mother Grey left the bicycle behind one of them and went on foot across the bridge, across the highway, and up the hill to the Fishersville flea market.

She was prepared to spend the whole morning finding her dishes. The rows of tables, some under long shed roofs, stretched across acres and acres, tables heavy with the fruit of many attics. Mud squished underfoot as she meandered between the displays, looking over the wares, listening to the dealers exchange complaints about the stinginess of the customers.

Plates aplenty were displayed in racks where she could admire their pretty patterns, but they were for collecting and showing off, not for eating. Something utilitarian, she thought. Something where all the dishes matched. She felt almost sorry for a table full of well-worn, grubby dolls of various sizes and ages, never again to be loved and played with now that they had been changed into collectibles.

Briefly she paused at a jewelry table whose merchandise was displayed in a locked glass case, old costume jewelry. She thought of the drawers she had had to go through after Granny's death. When she was little, Granny had let her play with some of the strings of beads. She didn't want to think about that, and so she moved on.

It was not her first visit to the Fishersville flea market, but since her chief interest was in dishes and cheap home furnishings, Mother Grey had never really noticed the other displays. This morning she was surprised at the number of war surplus tables, haunted as they were by strange young men in fatigues. She almost thought she saw Schwartz skulking in the Nazi memorabilia.

Then she nearly collided with Rochelle Hudson, dressed in a tight gray business suit and wearing her glamorous face paint—eye shadow, dark lipstick, and all. "Rochelle," she said. "Nice weather for shopping."

"I'm between appointments," she said. "I think the people I just showed a house to are going to buy. I'm celebrating."

"Congratulations. I'm here looking for some dishes."

"Marla told me she saw a mother-of-pearl-handled carving knife for sale here that matches my good carving fork. She thinks she saw it at that place up the side of the hill. Come with me; they have dishes up there too. Maybe you'll find what you want."

As they made their way through the crowd (where did all these people come from, on a Wednesday morning?), Mother Grey saw, she was sure of it now, the camouflage-clad form of Schwartz hunched over one of the tables. His collar was up, as though he were trying to make himself inconspicuous. With his gray-pale face and black beard stubble, he succeeded only in looking conspicuously sneaky. Some of the dealers were giving him a suspicious eye. *At least,* she thought, *he's out in the open air, away from that wretched computer.*

On second thought, maybe he was better off with the computer. As Mother Grey watched him, Schwartz sidled over to a table full of war surplus and began to feel the weapons. Her duty was clear; she must go to him and make herself known. Schwartz needed to understand that he was a part of a caring community, a community that would not permit him to wander around anonymously handling weapons, possibly even contemplating violent deeds.

By the time she caught up with him, he had grabbed hold of a large sharp knife with swastikas inlaid in the handle and was testing the blade on his thumb. "Hello, Schwartz," she said. He did not startle and cut himself. *I must be losing my touch,* she thought. She used to be able to speak in a voice of paralyzing authority. Perhaps she should do some more work with the tape recorder.

"Hi, Mother Vinnie."

"What are you doing?" she said, though she could see for herself he was fondling a knife.

"Looking to protect myself against the government."

"Schwartz, we are the government. This is a democracy."

"They'd like us to believe that, wouldn't they?"

"You're perfectly free to register to vote, Schwartz, and make your opinion felt at the polls like everyone else."

"No, actually, I'm not, Mother Vinnie. They won't let me. 'You can't vote, you're certifiably insane. You can't have a gun, you're certifiably insane. You can't get married, you're certifiably insane.' I tell you, I'm sick of it."

Could that be true? She would have to ask the town clerk about it. It might be another of Schwartz's delusions. The voting part, that is—not the part about having a gun or getting married. He probably shouldn't be doing either of those things. *Married?* "I didn't know you even had a girl, Schwartz," said Mother Grey.

"No point in it," he said. "Or so Danny tells me. But if I had a gun, you know, I could make my opinion felt in ways that really count."

"Don't be silly," she said to him. "Violence is never the answer."

"Depends on the question, doesn't it?" he said. "Ah, this looks more like it." He veered off toward another table, where handguns were laid out in neat rows. Presumably they were nonworking collectibles of some kind, and not the sort of firearms that Schwartz could pick up and use to register his views on the government.

Rochelle, trailing along behind her, said, "I know that guy. Who is he?"

"That's Schwartz. One of the disturbed young men from my halfway house."

"I remember him from the planning board meeting. Are you sure he's halfway?"

"He's making progress. You should have seen him two years ago. The Lord has done a great work in that man."

"I'll take your word for it, Mother Vinnie. Ah! There it is. Make believe you didn't see it." With an elaborate show of indifference, she seized the carving knife, almost hidden between two larger examples of its kind.

Mother Grey marveled at her keen eyesight. "How did you spot that?"

"Your eye gets trained," she said. "Tell me," she said to the dealer, "can you give me a better price on this?"

About that time Mother Grey saw the dishes of her dreams. They cost too much, but they were the same pattern as her grandmother's. Holding them took her back to Granny's sunny kitchen in Washington and the taste of warm banana bread. You can't put a price on that.

She realized that nostalgia was what they were selling here at the flea market—bits and pieces of people's lost youth. Still, practical or not, she wanted these dishes. *Dicker*, said a voice in her mind, perhaps the same Holy Spirit that gave her other good advice from time to time. She tried it out: "Can you do any better on the price?" The words felt alien on her lips, but the results were gratifying; the dealer knocked off fourteen percent. Wrapping them carefully in newspaper, she packed up the set in her backpack for the trip home, service for four with teacups and all.

As she made her way to the bush where the bike was hidden, she saw Dawn Hudson getting out of a yellow convertible. Dawn had washed the red dye out of her hair—very pretty hair it was in its natural state, light brown with highlights—but still her manner of dress made her look somehow like a streetwalker. *My word, her belly button is showing.* Well, it was a hot day after all, and tiny shorts and skimpy tops were the style. (But leather boots?)

A tall athletic youth with long hair and big heavy shoes got out of the driver's side of the car and crossed the road with her. It was Bunker Todd's son, the jet skier from the planning board meeting. Dawn seemed to be dragging him along on some furtive errand, now pulling him by the hand, now pushing down on his shoulder so that he might stay out of sight. Out of whose sight? They were hiding from someone, ducking behind things, behind tables or taller, wider people.

Mother Grey followed the line of the girl's interest and saw Rochelle.

So she was hiding from her mother, trying not to

be seen in the company of this perhaps undesirable boy. He did seem too old for Dawn, maybe eighteen or nineteen, and his face had the vacant look of the criminals in Mother Grey's favorite television show, *True Stories of Real Cops*. She had seen a face very like this boy's on a young drunk arrested for broadsiding a carload of orphans. Who, me? Responsible for anything? Rochelle probably didn't want Dawn seeing him, and no wonder. But if the couple wanted to avoid Rochelle, why were they creeping ever closer to the table where she stood concluding the transaction for the knife?

Children. There was no knowing why they did the things they did, especially adolescents, immature of judgment, half mad with raging hormones.

The bicycle was right where she had left it. She trundled it across the road and mounted up.

As she rode back into town, the paper-wrapped set of dishes bounced gently against her back. She thought of Granny, the flowered dishes, herself at fourteen. They used to have tea together when she came home from school. Still mourning Granddaddy's death ten years before, Granny used to wear black dresses, sometimes with a little white figure in them. Once a week she would make banana bread. After tea Vinnie would practice on her cello, the divine Weaver that had been her mother's.

It wasn't that long ago, twenty years or so, and yet what a different girl Vinnie had been from the girls of today—Dawn Hudson in particular. Vinnie would no more have exhibited her navel in public than she would have talked about men's bottoms. Well, times changed.

As Mother Grey rode along musing on these things, a loud bang echoed across the canal. She thought, *Someone is hunting the ducks*. The next sound she heard was a terrific splash.

"Does this washing machine work?"

Dave Dogg looked up from massaging his calf to behold a stout woman with bad teeth, glaring at him from the cab of a dark blue pickup truck with Pennsylvania plates. He was still pursuing his investigation on the borrowed police bike, because Kreevitch had said he might have it for another week, and because it was as good a way to get around town as any, but the exercise was getting to be too much. No sooner had he rubbed away the charley horse in his leg than the scavengers began to pester him. He was not here to give advice about trash washing machines.

"I wouldn't know anything about it," he said.

"Well, excuse *me*," she said, and drove down the block, where she stopped to check out some other stuff.

What did she take him for, a junk salesman? The bike trail along the canal would be a better way to get back to the parking lot where he had left his car. At least he could keep clear of trash hunters.

He tested his leg, which seemed to be recovered, mounted the bicycle, and headed north along the canal path. Sunlight sparkled on the surface of the deep muddy water. Bees buzzed in the purple flowers. Bees always seemed to like purple flowers. Birdsong, the soft muttering of ducks, and faraway music playing on a radio in someone's backyard. This was kind of nice. If it didn't make his legs so tired, it could be really great. Around the lumberyard, over the tracks. He monkeyed with the gears some more.

Geese on the trail by the Todds' house made a great squawking as Dave approached. When he leaned his bicycle against the house, the dogs began to bark. He could hear them clawing the front door when he went up the steps and rang the bell.

Apparently they did the same on the outside when they were out, since there were gouge marks the size of dog claws almost through the door paneling. Was anyone home? He rang the bell again.

At that moment the throb of superamplified heavy metal sounded, and the crunch of gravel, whereupon into the goose-infested yard roared a yellow 1963 Pontiac Bonneville with the top down. A nice piece of work, not a spot of rust on it, though Dave wasn't sure he approved of the hot-rod touches: orange flames painted on the fenders, oversize tires. A tall boy with long hair and big heavy shoes unfolded himself from the driver's seat and got out.

"Can I help you with something?" he said to Dave.

"I'm looking for Bunker Todd," Dave told him.

"My father's over at the construction site," the boy said, fitting his key into the lock. "He'll be back about six, maybe." The barking on the other side of the door reached a crescendo.

Dave showed him his shield. "May I talk to you for a minute?" he said. The boy opened the door; three Rottweilers surged around him. The boy got down on his hunkers and hugged them and rubbed their ears. "I don't know whether you heard about it, but one of your father's guns was used in a holdup last week," Dave said.

The boy stood up, hands on the dogs' collars. "Those were my guns," he said.

"They were?"

"The burglars never found my father's guns. What they stole were just target pistols, twenty-twos." The dogs looked at Dave in an unfriendly manner.

"Whatever they were, one of them killed a convenience store clerk."

"Sorry. They were registered and everything."

"I know. That's how we were able to trace this one; the killer dropped it, and then we had the number on file. Tell me something. Could you identify a cartridge casing if I showed it to you?"

"I could tell you whether it was a twenty-two, is all. Whether it was from my gun or not, no, I don't guess so."

"Just thought I'd ask. Do these look familiar?" He held out the bag with the shells from the hill. "Don't open it."

"Yeah, they look familiar. They're twenty-twos, they're brass, they could be from one of my pistols. Where'd you find them?"

"Various places in Fishersville," Dave said. He took the bag back and put it in his pocket. "Here's the thing, son. I think your other guns are still in town. I think a bunch of local kids took them, and I think they still have them."

"You think so?"

"I do. Maybe you can make a guess who the kids might be. Someone you know, maybe. It's not a very big town. Maybe you've had some suspicions, or someone has looked at you funny, like, 'Ha-ha, I have your guns.'"

"No. Sorry."

"You wouldn't have any idea at all?"

"No idea. I don't know what else to tell you."

Freddy and Garrett sat on the curb playing with bullets.

If you took a pair of pliers, you could get the front part of the bullet out and pour the gunpowder into a pile, or make a little trail; then when you set a burning match to it, things happened that were amazing and cool. Also you could use the powder to make rockets. "Don't forget to save the shells," said Garrett. "Chick showed me this really neat trick where you stick the shells in a bar of soap and punch out soap bullets."

"What good is that?"

"You can load them into the gun and shoot them."

"Do they hurt?"

"Oh, yeah. But the wound is real clean. I don't

know, do you think I'm stupid enough to shoot myself?"

"You were stupid enough to shoot Howie."

"That was an accident."

One of the neighbors had set a fancy old love seat out on the curb, the upholstery ripped and faded, the frame broken. A man drove up and stopped his car in front of it, leaving the engine running. Quickly the boys concealed the evidence of their bullet fun. As they watched him, he got out of the car and unscrewed the love seat's carved wooden arms.

He put the arms into the back of his car with the other stuff and drove on down the street, slowly. Freddy turned his attention to the rest of the trash.

"Hey, look at this." A hard black gritty semicircular object protruded from the box next to him. It turned out to be the tip end of an old skateboard. He wrenched it out of the box.

"Let me see," Garrett said.

"I saw it first," Freddy said. "It's mine." Why had such a treasure been thrown away? One wheel was loose, missing a screw. A simple matter of replacing it. He just happened to have a screw in his pocket; it just happened to fit. He tightened it down with his thumbnail, jumped on the skateboard, and set off to perform a thorough analysis of its capabilities.

"I'll go get mine and meet you back here," Garrett said. "We'll race them."

The best place for this sort of thing was the next street over, recently repaved, with new curbs, gutters, and storm drains. No traffic. Freddy cruised the length of the block a couple of times. When he felt he had his balance, he began swerving in and out of driveways.

Then he tried jumping the curb. He knew a guy who could jump two garbage cans on their sides, but he would start with the curb. It worked great!! Even better was the iron curb edge of the storm drain. He took a shot at it, and then another, perfecting his moves until he could jump into the air and land back on the skateboard with perfect timing.

Again and again he did the same thing perfectly. Maybe tomorrow he would be ready for jumping over garbage cans. Then one last time he happily hopped into the air, only to land on the sidewalk with no skateboard under him.

What the—?

The board, he realized, had slid out from under him and into the storm drain.

Cursing, he hunkered down and squinted into the darkness. The board was way down there. He couldn't reach it. He cursed again, louder this time.

Maybe he could get down in there. He had seen cats do it. His mother always said not to, because he could get stuck, or a flash flood could come and drown him. But it wasn't raining or anything. If he got stuck, he could just yell.

He couldn't do it headfirst, as it turned out, but when he started by putting his feet through the opening, he found that it wasn't all that hard, until it came time to get his head in. He had to turn it a certain way. Then he was all the way in, with only a slight scrape on one ear.

Of course he couldn't turn around. Actually he could barely move at all. And he couldn't really get out again. But that was okay; the pipe opening that drained into the canal was only seven or eight feet away. All he had to do was wiggle backward until he came out, with the skateboard underneath him. So maybe he would get his feet wet when he came out of the pipe. At least he would have this good skateboard back again.

He got himself on top of the skateboard with his toes pointed in the right direction. Enough light came through the grate for him to see the bottom of the sewer, slimy leaves and sticks from the last rain, paper cups and potato chip bags, cigarette butts, a condom. Then suddenly the biggest damned spider he had ever seen in his life looked him right in the eye. He cursed some more, quietly, hoping not to get it excited; it was about a foot from his nose.

Slowly he pushed himself backward.

As he put his hand out to find a purchase for getting himself further along, his hand closed around a long-barreled revolver. Another gun! If he'd known how easy it was to pick up guns, he would never have broken into that house. Good, Schwartz could have this one. He held it up in the little bit of light, where he could see it. Smell it too; smelled like it had been fired. Two empty chambers in the cylinder. He turned it so that a live round was up. That way maybe if a rat or like that came after him while he was down here, he would be all ready to shoot it.

Backward, backward toward the end of the pipe, ten more inches, twenty.

The spider was on the move too.

More stuff clogged the pipe than he would have thought—branches, trash, he couldn't see what, it was too dark. All he could see was a gray light under the grate and the silhouette of the spider, moving. It made a little run up the side of the pipe, incredibly fast, and then back again. Wolf spider. He'd heard about them once. Was it going to attack? He gripped the gun; maybe he could blast the spider.

Or maybe retreat was best. What if his bullets ricocheted? He could wind up like Howie, or worse. Backward another five feet. Slimy stuff, scuttling noises, something crawling on him. Then his toes felt the edge of the pipe. He was almost out.

But his clothes were stuck on something in the dark, branches, or claws. He began to yell for help.

Outside the pipe, strong hands grabbed his ankles.

For no reason he thought, *It's Rex.* In another second he would be able to see that one of the hands that had him by the legs was tattooed with a crude skull, and he would be able to hear Rex's old nasty laugh. Then Rex would pull him out of the sewer and hurt him some way. Rex, resurrected, like one of the skeleton warriors in the video game. You kill them and kill them, and they keep getting up. He took the gun in both his hands. *Try again.*

"Are you stuck, son?" The voice was not Rex's, but that of Coach Hudson. Good thing coach spoke to him. Freddy was all set to blow him away.

"Yes, I'm stuck," said Freddy. A splash; Coach must have got right into the water.

"Are you hurt?"

"No, sir."

"Good. I'm going to push you back in a little bit, and we'll see if we can get you unhooked." It worked; Coach pulled him out like a cork from a bottle and set him on dry land, skateboard and all. Spiders were crawling all over his pants, but Coach got the spiders off before Freddy screamed too much.

"What's this?" Coach said, noticing the revolver in his fist.

"I found it in there," Freddy said.

Coach stood back and gave him a funny look; Freddy couldn't read it. He guessed he was mad at him for going in the sewer. Good catchers weren't all that easy to find.

"Don't ever go in there again."

"No, sir. I don't guess I will."

"Better let me have that," Coach said, and took the gun away from him.

It was all the same. Freddy still had his other one back in the cello case. Too bad for Schwartz, but since they seemed to be lying around all over the place, maybe he could find his own gun.

8

D ave got back on the bike and headed southward, toward the parking lot where his car
was. The smooth flat gravel path gave out
abruptly. Engineering problems or expense had
halted the trail's development, and it ran along un-
finished for several blocks, a hazardous ride, narrow,
weedy, and bumpy. Before the state canal commission finished this stretch of the bike path, the bank
itself would need to be built out and shored up; the
walls of these old buildings came almost to the canal
bank. Dave thought, *Maybe I'll take the street*. But a
path continued on, and though it was scarcely wider
than the tires of his bike, it bore the tracks of somebody's tires.

He thought of the sparkle sharks prowling the
rubbish of the town, waiting to harass him, and decided to chance it. If worse came to worst and he fell
in, he could always swim. Too bad for Kreevitch's
police bike.

At the first curve he came to, Dave was forced to stop and dismount; Lavinia Grey was standing in the path, staring into the canal. Something with small fat wheels lay on its side in the brown water, a dark green golf cart, half submerged.

"What's up?" he said.

She said, "I think this just went in."

"Anybody driving?"

"I don't know. I didn't see it happen. I heard a splash." They both peered into the water; it was much too muddy to see anything.

By the golf cart a large stump grew out of the canal bank, one of its knobby roots protruding into the path. "The trail doesn't even look wide enough to drive one of those things here," Dave said. "Maybe one of the wheels got caught on this root."

"They aren't allowed on the trail anyway," she said. "Motorized vehicles." She was poking up and down among the bushes on the bank.

There was no puddle to mark where a person might have come out of the water. Of course it might have been that no one was aboard when it went in. Hopefully that was the case—maybe it was the kid gang again, stealing a golf cart and driving it into the canal. Who would drive a thing like this on the bike path anyway, except kids? Who would even own one? The nearest golf course was ten miles away.

But what if some kid had gone in with it and was even now down under the mud?

"Take this and call for help," he said, handing her his cellular phone. "I'll see what I can find down there. I was a lifeguard once." He pulled off his shoes and shirt and scrambled down the bank. As he hit the water, he ripped his arm a good one on the blackberry thorns.

Diving and diving again, he groped all around the cart, then down into the very bottom of the canal. Nothing. Every time he put his head out of the water, he saw Vinnie on the bank, wringing her hands. He heard the siren; help was on its way, but time was passing. Whoever came would come too late.

Dave had been in the water a good ten minutes by the time the professional divers arrived with a rowboat, wetsuits, and tanks. He hauled out and sat on the bank, taking in air. There was water in his eyes, and his arm stung.

"You're bleeding," Vinnie said.

"I want to stay here till they find whoever it is."

"Maybe it's nobody," she said. "Maybe it's all for nothing. Why don't you come home with me and let me fix your arm?"

Kreevitch came scrambling up the bank. "In a minute," Dave said.

Vinnie looked at his arm again. "You should clean this cut," she said.

"Ah, it's just mud," he said. "The Indians used to use it to dress wounds."

"I'll get the car and come back for you," she said, leaving. Poor Vinnie. She didn't want to be there when they pulled the blue corpse of some kid out of the water.

With a scrape and a splash the underwater search team launched the boat. There were three of them, two divers in black and yellow wetsuits and a guy to man the rowboat. The divers slipped in after it. Starting where the cart had gone in, they slowly moved downstream, holding a thick nylon rope between them. Kreevitch watched them work, his hands on his hips.

"What's the rope for?" Dave said.

"Beats the hell out of me. Maybe to snag the body, or to keep track of the other diver in the mud."

"I thought you would know the drill."

"We don't get a lot of drownings this end of the canal," said Kreevitch. "Fourteen years on the Fishersville police force, and I never saw one. The river, yes. Or the wing dam, with those stupid canoers trying the rapids. What I can't figure out is where the hell this golf cart came from."

"Some golfer in town," Dave said.

"No motorized vehicles allowed on this trail. Damned thing doesn't even fit—anybody could see that," Kreevitch said.

"What about old Horace Burkhardt, that guy who lives next to Vinnie? He plays golf. He talks all the time about how much golf he's going to play when he gets to St. Augustine."

"So he does," Kreevitch said.

"Does he have any enemies?"

"Only the entire youth baseball league," Kreevitch said. "Maybe one of the coaches dumped the old guy in the canal."

"How many coaches are there?"

"About twenty," Kreevitch said. "Counting me."

The two divers surfaced and with a splash went

down again. Dave and Kreevitch watched them; it was like watching dolphins cavorting in chocolate pudding.

Presently the amiable Morris Chasen from the *Clarion* came strolling down the trail, camera in hand. "What's going on?" he said.

"Golf cart in the water," said Kreevitch.

"Whose is it?"

"Don't know."

"Any theories?"

"None whatever," Kreevitch lied.

Chasen began to take pictures of the cart.

In the rectory Mother Grey took her backpack to the kitchen table and carefully unpacked four dinner plates, four bread and butter plates, four cups, and four saucers. All had made the journey safely. Later on, when everything was normal, when those who searched the canal had come up empty and the golf cart proved to have been dumped in as a prank . . . later on, when Dave Dogg had gone away from Fishersville again, back to his little family . . . later on, she would make banana bread. *Dear Lord, let it be all right*. If they hadn't found anyone in the water yet, probably there was no one to find. No old men, no mischievous children growing cold and stiff down under the mud.

Maybe next year she would learn to cook. Then she could have a dinner party, invite three other people. Or even sooner. Maybe Horace would like to come to dinner. In her mind she saw the old man rolling along the canal bank on a golf cart, bumping the tree root, falling in.

But Horace didn't have a golf cart, at least not that she'd ever seen. It couldn't have been him. Just the same, it might be a good idea to look in on him before she went to fetch Dave Dogg, who claimed to be perfectly comfortable sitting on the canal bank waiting for bodies to come up.

She went over and knocked on Horace's door. Dead silence within.

Maybe he was in the motor home, still parked in his driveway, poised for flight to Florida. Its air conditioner was running noisily, and through the walls came the faint strains of big band jazz—Stan Kenton, she thought. She knocked on the door of the motor home, but no one answered there either.

Either the old man was still out, or he was hiding. *Horace needs his privacy,* she said to herself. She would let him alone. If he was in there and not at the bottom of the canal.

She got in the car and went to pick up Dave. He was sitting where she had left him. Jack Kreevitch was pacing up and down the canal bank, now poking in the weeds, now pausing to watch the divers.

"Have they found anything?" she said.

"No bodies yet," Dave said. "They found a golf hat in the water."

"Why don't you come with me?" she said. "I'll drive you to the emergency room."

"No."

"I think you should," she said. "I think your arm needs stitches."

"No stitches," he said.

"Come home with me, then, and let me dress it. I have some first aid supplies." He got into the car, still dripping canal water and bleeding from his arm. She took him to the rectory and made him sit down in the kitchen.

Her supplies were still laid out from the morning. "What's this?" he said.

"Butterfly bandages and hydrogen peroxide," she said. "It won't sting, and if it does, you just breathe in and out very fast." She took a hot washcloth and began to clean the arm around the cut.

"You want me to do Lamaze breathing for a cut on my arm?" Dave said.

"Lamaze breathing. Is that what it is? Someone told me once to do it for pain. It works pretty well. If it doesn't, you can pinch yourself on the ear." She swabbed the wound with peroxide-soaked cotton. Lamaze breathing. That would be one of the million memories he shared with his wife, from when Ricky was born.

"Ow," he said.

"Pinch, pinch, pinch. All done." She taped a gauze dressing over the wound, being careful not to tape over the pretty little red hairs that curled out of the freckled skin of his arm. When he pulled the bandage off it would hurt less that way. Or when Felicia pulled it off. Whoever.

Practice was making her good at this butterfly bandage business, which was what you could do sometimes instead of stitches. Earlier it had been Howie Reeker, bleeding from the earlobe. She knew there was some good reason why children shouldn't be allowed to pierce their ears, and sure enough he had had some stupid accident with his earring that had torn a big hole clear through it. Naturally he had come to Mother Grey, the way all the other stray dogs did. Nobody wanted to go to the emergency room anymore. She was less surprised about Howie's aversion to doctors and stitches than about Dave's. "What a baby you are," she said. "Don't you ever get hurt in the line of duty?"

"Sure don't," he said. "You've been watching television again, I see."

"I just thought getting shot and stuff was part of the job."

"Happens about as often as a minister getting a personal visit from Satan. Which is to say sometimes, right? But we avoid it whenever we can."

"Quite so. Now, what about your wet clothes?" she said.

"I thought I'd just take them off and sit here naked."

Right, and then I can take your shorts outside and hang them on the line in front of all Fishersville. "I still don't have a dryer," she said. "With all the things people have given me for deductions on their taxes, a dryer has never yet come my way. Actually I'm just as glad. If you hang them out on the line, the clothes will dry by themselves. Patience is a good Christian virtue." It was like the pretzels. For what was wholesome you had to wait.

"You always talk a lot, don't you, when you're waiting for someone to make a pass at you."

"I'm not waiting for you to make a pass at me. I don't want you to make a pass at me." It was important to make this clear. "I don't want to get back into that kind of relationship with you, Dave. I'm very serious about this."

"Why not? Let's go upstairs, and I'll take my wet clothes off. Towser won't mind."

Why not, indeed. For a thousand reasons, none of which was that she found him unattractive. In the first place, the man had a wife at home, whether or not they had gotten around to remarrying.

At last she said what her grandmother would have said: "It's not done." She would be okay if she didn't look at his eyes, remarkably blue, remarkably hypnotic.

"It's done all the time, Vinnie."

By ordinary people. "Not by me."

She thought sure he was going to kiss her anyway, but suddenly Towser jumped up with a rattle of toenails and gave a bark. He was answered by a knock on the back door.

There stood Mac Barrow. "Come in," she said to him.

Mac seemed about to say something until he saw Dave sitting at the table with no shirt on. Then he blinked and, as it seemed, deliberately cleared his face of all expression. So Mac Barrow was offended at the sight of Dave half naked in her kitchen. How starchy he was. Mac took a breath and started again: "Jack Kreevitch sent me over here. He thought you'd want to know. They found the body."

It wasn't as though they weren't expecting to

hear this. Still, there was a moment of stunned silence.

"Drowned?" said Dave.

"Shot," Mac replied. "Dead when he hit the water, the medics figured."

Poor Horace! At least Mother Grey wouldn't have to bury him, cast out by the Roman church for making away with himself. And no one could say he hadn't lived to a ripe old age. But shot? Who could have shot him? One of the Little League coaches? Or . . .

Towser jumped up and barked at the kitchen door again. Framed in the screen door, the ghostly face of the supposed victim peered in at them. "My word," Mother Grey murmured, and put her hand to her heart. The specter began to bang on the door.

"Come on in, Horace," said Dave. The old man came in, very much alive, not even wet.

"I'm out of food for my daughter's dog," he said, shutting the door behind him. "That animal eats like a horse. Can you let me have three or four cans of dog food, Mother Vinnie, until I can get to the store tomorrow?"

"Certainly," she said. "I have some kibble too if you want it."

Then Horace noticed the men in her kitchen, Dave still with no shirt on. "Hello, there," he said.

"Horace, this is Mac Barrow, and of course you know Dave."

"Mac Barrow! *The* Mac Barrow? How about that."

Mac Barrow said, "Good evening, sir," and shook his hand.

"What's going on?" Horace said. "The way you all look, you'd think something terrible happened."

"There's been an accident," Mother Grey said.

"Anyone killed?"

"Bunker Todd," Mac said. "They found his body in the canal just now."

Horace started, quivering as though from an electric shock. "Bunker Todd is dead!"

"I'm afraid so," Mac said.

"Then I'm out of the contract!" Horace said.

"If that's how it works, then yes, I guess you are," Mac said.

"Hot damn!" he cried. "Hallelujah!" And he took a couple of little capering dance steps. Suddenly his legs folded under him, and he dropped to the floor like a sack of bones.

Mother Grey knelt down beside him and chafed his hands. "Horace," she called softly. He moaned and thrashed around, but he didn't answer.

Dave called an ambulance, using his cellular phone.

"He's unconscious," Mother Grey said.

"They're on the way," Dave said. The two men stood around awkwardly, waiting. After a minute Dave put his shirt back on and buttoned it up.

9

Danny Handleman carried the tidings of the murder of Bunker Todd from Delio's to the halfway house, or to Schwartz, since their roommate Frank was still locked up in the Medical Center. "Bunker Todd's body was just found in the canal," he said. "The news is flying all over town like a greased pig." Schwartz was peeling potatoes in preparation for one of his manly meals.

"Couldn't be a pig, man," Schwartz said. "Pigs can't fly."

"A greased buzzard, then." They meditated for a while on the image of a greased buzzard circumnavigating Fishersville, trumpeting bad news.

Schwartz picked up the peeler and resumed scraping. "It's perfectly clear to me who's responsible," he said.

"You knew Bunker Todd?"

"I didn't have to know him," Schwartz said. "I only have to know the way the world works. Remember the planning board hearing I told you about? That was Bunker Todd. Here he was, a free man, exercising his God-given property rights, and the ZOG agent shot him down."

"The ZOG agent," Danny repeated, as if he hadn't heard it a hundred times before.

"The ZOG agent. Zionist Occupation Government. The park ranger. He wears this uniform, with the hat and everything. Brown shirt. Very significant."

"Ever since you've been on the Internet with those right-wing nuts, you are getting to be such an asshole, Schwartz. Listen to me. There is no Zionist Occupation Government. It's a figment of your right-wing nut friends' imagination."

"You'll see, Danny. Just wait. Next come the black helicopters, the jack-booted troops. I'm telling you, we have to get ready. Put on a pot of water to boil for me, will you?"

"Do it yourself," Danny said. "I'm cooking tomorrow."

"Oh, yeah, right. What's it going to be this time, tofu helper or Egg Beaters and bean sprouts? I wish to hell Frank would get out."

"Just tell me one thing, Schwartz," Danny said. "If the Jews are taking over the world, why haven't I heard anything about it? I mean, I'm Jewish. Where's my piece?"

"You don't understand, Dan. This is bigger than your average Jew on the street. This is international bankers. This is the UN."

"Oh, excuse me, the UN. I thought you were saying Jews. You know, we Jews are kind of sensitive about talk like that. Like, I lost two great-uncles and a whole bunch of second cousins at a place called Auschwitz because of talk like that."

"That's their story," said Schwartz. His eyes were a little wilder than usual, and it occurred to Danny that he might be on the edge of an episode. Great, just great. Danny wondered if there mightn't be some way he could get him to take his medication without knowing it—dissolve it in his coffee maybe. Coffee was a manly drink; Schwartz would chug that down without much caring what it tasted like. He rinsed out the coffee pot and prepared to make a fresh batch.

"So the park ranger murdered Bunker Todd, in order to . . . in order to do what?" Danny asked, measuring a hefty hit of coffee grounds. The bitterer it was, the more it would disguise the taste. "Why would he do that? I thought he'd already made his point at the hearing. Bunker Todd lost. It seems to me that if anybody murdered anybody, it would be the other way around." He set the pot to perking and looked around for Schwartz's pill bottle.

"Opportunity," Schwartz said. "Picture this. Here comes the brownshirt, patrolling the canal path in his jackboots. Who should he see but Bunker Todd, the free man, defenseless and alone. He mustn't be allowed to live. The brownshirt draws his trusty ZOG sidearm, and blooey! He blows him away."

"I don't think park rangers carry sidearms," said Danny. "I could be wrong." There it was, on top of the refrigerator. Now, how to get a pill out without Schwartz noticing? "Hey, look, I think I see him," Danny said. "Down by the canal path. He's looking at our house." While Schwartz rushed to the window, Danny deftly secured a dose of his medication behind his back.

"I don't see anybody," said Schwartz.

"My mistake," said Danny.

"But you know something, they have a clear field of fire from that canal bank to our house. They can take us anytime."

"Do you really think so?"

"Yeah, look here." Schwartz drew him by the shoulder to the window over the sink, where the two gazed outward. Schwartz gestured at the yard with outspread fingers. "All they need is one machine-gun emplacement, right there at the steps by the canal bank, to command the yard and the house and everything. They have us."

What is real? What is not? For an instant Danny could see the whole setup just as Schwartz was describing it to him, the shadows of occupation troops lurking beyond the hedge, peeping up over the steps, the tops of their helmets just visible. Or were those the garden lights?

"What you want to do is put sandbags," said Schwartz.

There came a loud rattling knock on the screen door, and for an instant Danny thought, *They're here.* But it was only Freddy Kane and some kid with blue hair, jewels in his nose, and a bandage on his ear.

Schwartz let them in. Danny busied himself with

setting out coffee mugs and stirring Schwartz's pills into the one on the left.

Freddy was making introductions. "This is Schwartz. Schwartz, this is, um, my friend. I wanted him to meet you. Because of what we talked about."

"Hail, friend," Schwartz said. "Would you like some coffee?"

"No, thank you," said Freddy.

"A man's drink. It'll put hair on your chest."

"I don't want hair on my chest, thanks," Freddy said, but his friend said, sure, he'd have a cup, and Danny had to get another mug down and fill it. It was then that he became confused about which mug he had put the medication into.

He thought, *I'll create some sort of diversion, knock over all the mugs, and start fresh,* but even as he was forming this plan, the other two grabbed mugs at random and began to drink. Ah, well, too late now. What would be would be. The odds were one in three that Schwartz got the right mug anyhow.

"What we talked about?" Schwartz said. "Oh, yeah. Right."

The two boys exchanged glances, then looked at Schwartz, then all three of them looked at Danny. Danny stirred some sugar into the remaining mug, added a splash of milk, and began to drink. It tasted normal.

Almost.

Suddenly he began to feel funny.

"We gotta go," said Freddy. "My mom will be home in a couple of minutes."

"Go in peace, my son," said Schwartz. "We'll talk later. By the way, I don't suppose you've noticed any unusual activity in the area of the canal."

"No," said Freddy.

"Cops, is all," said the other boy. "Down by Ash Street. But that's because of the murder."

"Still," said Schwartz. "Government agents." He squinted at Danny. "Mark it well, Danny."

"The cool thing was the helicopter," Freddy said.

Schwartz sat up straight. "What color was it?"

"Black," the boys said together.

"And what was it doing?"

"Just flying around," said Freddy.

"What did I tell you, Danny?" said Schwartz. "Mark it well."

The boys gave him a strange look. "Bye," said Freddy. They left, banging the screen door behind them.

A curious feeling of inner peace warmed Danny's vitals. Schwartz's words were beginning to sound almost sensible to him. He thought, *The ranger killed Bunker Todd, a free citizen, and next he'll come after us.* But the thought did not frighten or even particularly move him.

"Black helicopters," Schwartz said. "Here in Fishersville."

"Black helicopters," Danny said. "You think this means invasion?"

"There are thirteen hundred people in my Internet newsgroup, and all of them know what's coming. Did you think that many guys could be mistaken?"

"What are you going to do?"

"About what?" said Schwartz.

"About Bunker Todd. About the ranger killing him."

"Oh, that. Nothing. Why should I interfere with events in Fishersville? It's nothing to do with me. I plan to join my brothers in the militia in Idaho as soon as I can cash my next SSI check."

This seemed wrong to Danny somehow, for Schwartz to abandon Fishersville in the middle of all this. If the government was actually murdering innocent citizens, something should be done about it. "What about justice?" said Danny. "What about doing the right thing?"

"We can bring justice to Fishersville later."

"I don't think it's right for you to just leave, knowing what you know," Danny said.

"What would you do?"

Danny shrugged. What would be the appropriate thing to do? "Struggle against tyranny."

"Hm." Schwartz appeared to consider Danny's proposal, frowning and stroking his beard for a long time. "You know, you're right," he said at last. "Armed struggle. I like it."

The sandbags were up to Freddy's nose the next morning when he got to the halfway house. On his way there he went through the bushes and down by the canal, the way he did every morning, figuring if Rex or somebody tried to sneak up and get him, he would hear them rustling in the underbrush. So far he had been safe. He really liked the sandbags. Schwartz must be playing army again.

He found him in the kitchen, lingering over the last morsels of breakfast—canned corned beef hash and a fried egg. Yum. Schwartz's day to cook.

"Is there any more of that?" Freddy asked him.

"Pan on the stove." Schwartz was doodling with a pad and pencil. It looked as though he were making football strategies.

"What's that?" Freddy said. He could take fried eggs or leave them alone, but half a can of corned beef hash was still in the skillet, greasy and crispy-brown on the bottom.

"A contingency plan. You will have noticed the improved fortifications between here and the canal."

"Yeah, the sandbags," Freddy said, scraping the hash onto a plate. "Do I need to save any of this for Danny?"

"He ate," Schwartz said. "See, I'm trying to improve the field of fire."

"You mean you have something to shoot?"

"No, no. That will come later."

"Because that's why I brought that kid over here yesterday, so you could see what he looks like. He wants to meet you someplace, but he doesn't want you to know his name."

"It's forgotten already," Schwartz said.

"I don't think he ever told it to you."

"Why doesn't he want me to know his name?"

"So you can't identify him in case something goes wrong."

"But I can always call him the kid with the

spiked blue hair. There aren't that many in Fishersville."

"I'm just saying what he told me to tell you."

"What are we talking about, anyway? What could go wrong? Who cares if I identify him?"

"He wants to sell you a gun."

"Ah." Schwartz put the pencil down.

"If I tell you this, Schwartz, you have to promise never to tell anybody."

"I am nothing if not discreet," said Schwartz, and placed a finger to his lips. It was true that as far as Freddy knew, Schwartz had never told any of his secrets. He might as well tell him everything. Except Howie's name, of course.

"How—ah—this kid got shot in the ear with his brother's twenty-two, so he stole it away from him, and now he wants to sell it."

"I don't know about a twenty-two," Schwartz said.

"But this is, like, an automatic. It's black. You'll like it."

"I'd rather have an AK-47."

"So would he."

"What does he want for it?"

"Do you have fifty dollars?"

Schwartz reached in his pocket, pulled out a roll of greasy money, and counted it slowly. "Sure," he said. "Here."

"No, you have to give it to him," said Freddy. Howie had been very specific about his plans. "He said you should meet him in the cannon park in half an hour, behind the statue of the Civil War soldier."

"Let me get this straight," said Schwartz. "This is the kid who was here yesterday, right? The one with the spiked hair and the gold things stuck in his nose. But he doesn't want me to know his real name."

"Right."

"Okay," said Schwartz. "I'll just call him Spike. Tell him I'll be there."

Just as she was about to take Towser out for his morning ramble, Mother Grey's telephone rang. It was Saraleigh.

"What's up?"

"I've been thinking about what we talked about yesterday," Saraleigh said.

"Freddy?"

"Yeah. He slept with his cello case again last night. I think you're right, Mother Vinnie. Something is going on with that kid."

"Maybe he should talk to someone. If you like, I can give you the name of a good child psychologist. Your health insurance from the paper bag factory would probably pick up most of the cost."

"Don't got no insurance. I pay the doctor out of my pocket. I only been working there four months."

"No insurance?"

"You remember how it was with Ralphie. You have to work there six months before they give you benefits."

"What about Ralph's new job, then? Doesn't his uncle . . ."

"I'll have to ask him when he gets home. Maybe

the kid does need a shrink. He keeps thinking he sees Rex Perskie."

"That could easily be," Mother Grey said. "I saw him myself only yesterday."

"You saw Rex?" Scritch, puff, whiff. "What was he doing?"

"Come to think of it, he was talking to Bunker Todd."

Saraleigh laughed, coughing a little. "I like it," she said. "Go find Jack Kreevitch, and tell him what you just told me. Let them fry Rex for murdering Bunker Todd. That will solve a whole bunch of my problems."

"Right. I will. But in the meantime, maybe you should keep Freddy indoors, at least until Rex is in custody."

"Can't. He has to go to the ball field. Today is the Angels' last game before the play-offs. I can't even be there, Britney has an ear infection, and the only appointment I could get was about halfway into the first inning."

"Maybe I can go and keep an eye on him, then," Mother Grey said, trying to think how she could do that and everything else she had to do too.

"How about you working the shack?"

"Working the shack?"

"It's my day to do it. I tried to call Rochelle—she's the team mother, she's supposed to get me a substitute. But nobody answers over there."

"Do you think I'm qualified to do it?"

"Just for maybe half an hour, until we get back from the doctor's. You could watch the game. Freddy would love to have you there. That way you could see that he was all right."

How could she refuse? "But what do I have to do?"

"Rochelle will fill you in."

"All right, then," she said, and they bade one another good-bye. Towser, for his part, could wait no longer, so she clipped his lead on, and they went out into the warm sunny morning.

As they walked past the cannon park, she noticed Jack Kreevitch stooping beside the Civil War soldier, fiddling with his bike. He wore his official bicycle policeman uniform: tight pants that showed off the muscles in his legs, and a black shirt with POLICE written across the back in seven-inch yellow letters.

"Good morning, Jack," she called.

" 'Lo, Mother Vinnie," he said.

"What's new?"

"Nothin' much. Looking for runaway kids this morning, is all. You haven't seen my niece, have you?"

"Not since yesterday. Is she missing?"

"Didn't come home last night. Rochelle is pretty upset. I have a feeling she's just gone off with one of her friends. Kids. What's new with you?"

"If you can imagine it, some big dog made a mess on my front steps yesterday. No sooner do I get the bad words scrubbed off than dogs begin to use my steps for a bathroom."

Kreevitch blushed. "Wasn't our dog, Mother Vinnie. Marla always picks up after him."

He knows more than he's telling. "Sheila Dresner told me she saw three policemen and a dog yesterday on the rectory doorstep."

"She did? She see who they were?"

"But that's not what I wanted to talk to you about. I saw Rex Perskie yesterday."

He put the bicycle wrench down. "No kidding," he said.

"He was talking to Bunker Todd. It was only about an hour before Todd was shot."

"How did you know he was shot?"

"Mac told me. You sent him to my house, remember?"

"Oh, yeah. Right."

"Was it supposed to be a secret?"

"Well, you know how the county prosecutor's office is," he said. "They don't want anything to get out that doesn't have to get out. Don't let it go any further."

"So. Do they have any leads?"

"Where did you see him talking to Rex?"

"It was down by those houses he's building. Is this evidence or something? Do you want a statement?"

"I'll have the county detective get back to you. Rex is back, is he? Man." He shook his head, as though to say, *What a fool, to come back here after everything that happened.*

"And Freddy Kane thinks somebody is following him around. That might be Rex. Can you keep an eye on him? Saraleigh too. I worry about them, with Ralph away in the Midwest."

"Those two can take care of themselves better than you think," said Kreevitch.

"Just the same."

"Okay, Mother Vinnie," he said. "I promise I'll keep an eye out."

"And I'll keep an eye out for Dawn Hudson," she said. "Say hi to Marla for me." She and Towser traveled onward, from tree to fire hydrant. There was something useful she almost remembered about Dawn—when Mother Grey saw her last, she was—but here came Schwartz, skulking along toward the park with such a furtive look that it knocked whatever Mother Grey was about to think of right out of her head.

"Mother Vinnie," he muttered, by way of greeting.

"Hi, Schwartz," she said.

He looked toward the park, saw the uniformed Officer Kreevitch rattling his bicycle and kicking the tires, and started guiltily. "You haven't seen me," he said. He turned around and walked the other way.

10

Freddy slipped through the bushes, performing the last of a series of evasive maneuvers he had worked out to shake off pursuit. Already he had cut through some backyards around by the canal bank, climbed a fence, and gone in the back and out the front of Rocco LaRosa's garage.

Because today he was certain that somebody was after him. The times he turned to look he saw no one, it was true, but there were shadows behind trees that shouldn't have been there, and once he heard a man clear his throat.

From the roof of Roscoe Hanks's shed, Freddy could plainly see that whoever had been after him wasn't anywhere around. He got down and ran to the front door of his apartment building, tiptoed up the stairs, and let himself in by the key around his neck.

"Mom?" he called. She wasn't home yet. He locked all three of the locks and bolts behind him.

He'd better get the pistol ready. He opened the

cello case and slipped it out of the pocket that it shared with his resin and tuning pipes. If he was going to have to shoot Rex, he needed to make sure this gun was clean and in good working order. It would be bad if it misfired.

He took the book from under his mattress, the one on how to maintain your Ruger double-action revolver, which he had borrowed from the library. Mother Vinnie was right; reading was a wonderful thing, you could find out all kinds of useful information. It was important to make sure it was unloaded before you did anything, and so he carefully took out all the bullets.

He had the pistol in pieces and was oiling them when a loud knock sounded at the front door. Freddy pulled a chair up and looked out through the special magnifying peephole.

It was Rex all right. He was smoking a cigarette and jigging from one foot to the other like he wanted to come in and use the bathroom. Of course Freddy wasn't going to let him in. But would he go away after a while? Or would he try to break the door down again? Freddy's mom had gotten the landlord to make the doors stronger after the last time, but still they hadn't been tested; maybe Rex could still get in. He seemed determined; he began to curse and hammer on the door with the side of his fist.

"Wait till I get this gun back together," Freddy muttered, fitting the pieces together with clumsy fingers. There was too much oil. He needed to wipe some of it off. Where was that rag?

Then suddenly Rex stopped pounding. Back at

the peephole, Freddy saw him looking over his tattooed shoulder. Footsteps were coming up the stairs.

Freddy hoped it wasn't his mom. If it was, he would have to open the door, and then Rex might get inside the apartment before the gun was ready.

Who it was, though, was Coach Hudson. Freddy could hear his voice through the door.

"Rex, ol' buddy," he said. "What are you doing here?"

"Came to see my kid," Rex said.

"Maybe you'd better come by later, when you sober up."

"I got a right to see my own kid."

Lies. "No he doesn't, Coach. My mom has a court order," Freddy called through the door. "He's not supposed to come around here at all."

"I'll get you later, you little bastard!" Rex hollered back.

"Let's take a walk," Coach said to Rex. Coach Hudson was the bigger of the two. As they went down the stairs together, Coach put his arm around Rex, but not in a friendly way; he seemed to be almost pushing him. The street door slammed, and Freddy ran to the window. He watched them go all the way down the street and into town. From time to time Rex looked back over his shoulder.

Cook the hot dogs, roast the pretzels, make the coffee, sell the drinks and snacks, and later on put out the soda for the players; the duties of the shack seemed simple enough, the way Rochelle explained them.

"I'm going home," Rochelle said. "I'll come back later and help you with cleanup." She looked quite ill.

"Are you okay?" Mother Grey said. "I can take care of all this if you want to stay home and get some rest."

"Don't worry about me," she said. "I'll see you later." She left as Garrett and some of the other players came to the shack window to stock up on Big League Chew.

"Is your mother all right, Garrett?" Mother Grey asked him.

"My stupid sister ran away last night."

"So I heard. No word yet where she is?"

"No. I'm just as glad. I hope she's gone to California or someplace. But my mother is pretty upset."

"I'm sorry to hear it," Mother Grey said. "Tell her to let me know if there's anything I can do."

The crowd of children dissipated; there stood Dave Dogg.

"Gimme a Nutty Buddy," he said. She looked at the price sheet. She found the price for a Nutty Buddy, all right, but she didn't know what in the world it was. "It's in the ice cream case," he said. "You never did this before, did you?"

"No," she said.

"How about I come in there and help you?"

"You don't have to do that."

He came in the door. "It'll be a good place for me to hang out," he said. "I need to be here."

"You're working, aren't you."

"I'm always working," he said. "Crime never sleeps." He opened the freezer case. "See?" he said. "Nutty Buddy." The range of merchandise in the freezer case was enormous, from pizza slices to red and blue things shaped like rockets on a stick.

She said, "I myself am here to keep an eye on Freddy." Freddy was in the dugout, though, and she couldn't see it from where she was.

"Why?"

"Saraleigh told me he thinks someone is following him," she said.

"Interesting," Dave said, in that tone of voice that always froze her blood.

"What do you mean?"

"I'm fairly certain that our boy Fred was involved in the gun burglary."

"Oh, no, Dave."

"Here's the story. Keep it to yourself, okay? They found an Angels team baseball cap at the scene. It had to belong to a kid. The tabs were adjusted to fit a small head. Five of the little Angels, including Freddy, have heads the right size, two of them girls. The other two boys were in day camp at the time. I can't see girls doing house burglaries."

"What a sexist you are," she said.

He shrugged. "We work with probabilities and profiles," he said. "That ain't sexism, it's modern forensic science."

"So what are you going to do?"

"First of all, I'm going to see who his friends are.

And then if someone is following him, I'm going to find out who and why."

A growing crowd waited outside the shack window, and they broke off their discussion to serve the customers. What worked best was for Mother Grey to call out the requests and take the money and Dave to find the treats. He at least knew whether a Jolly Rancher was frozen, cooked, dispensed from the soda machine, or stored in the candy rack.

Mother Grey had to be firm at times about taking each customer in turn. Sometimes no more was visible than a pair of small hands grasping the edge of the counter, one small hand clutching some sticky coins or a dollar bill. Then she would lean out of the window, look down, and say, "May I help you?" very solemnly. The tiniest children always asked for the most unwholesome items.

After five or six small customers, she found herself looking at a large brass belt buckle decorated with a fierce muscular eagle.

"Why, hello, Schwartz," said Mother Grey. "It's nice to see you."

"Mother Vinnie. Greetings."

"What brings you to the ball game?"

"Patriotism," said Schwartz. "I'm here to celebrate the American Dream. Let me have a couple of those. Blue ones, if you can find them." He pointed to a jar of wrapped hard candy. While she fished for blue ones, he said, "Actually I came with Danny. He wants to watch Freddy play. By the way, you haven't seen my friend Spike, have you? He's this kid with spiked hair and jewelry in his nose."

"Not unless you mean one of the Reeker boys," she said. "I saw Howie a while ago. Why?"

"No reason," he said. "Reeker?"

"One of them calls himself Howie. The other is Chick." There were more of them, but these two were the ones she knew who were currently in town.

"Reeker. Good," he said. "By the way, you didn't hear me ask."

"Anything you say, Schwartz." She took his money and gave the candy to him. "Mind you don't give any of this garbage to Freddy," she said. "Or Danny. Neither one of them can afford the dental work. You can't either," she called after his back. "You might think about that."

"Now, Mom, stop nagging," Dave said.

"The water isn't even fluoridated here," she said. "These poor children are sitting ducks for dental caries." The next person in line was a boy who wanted to know what she had sold his friend to turn his tongue that color, because he wanted some too. His friend, standing next to him, grinned and displayed his bright-green tongue but refused to name the candy that had done it. Mother Grey herself couldn't remember.

"How about one of these?" she said. He bought it and went away happy; she felt like a pusher for sugar and aniline dye.

When the crowd had thinned, she realized that the game was already in progress, the Angels were in the field, and Freddy, encumbered by fifty pounds of protective equipment, was in his appointed place behind home plate. Safe enough for now.

What if Freddy had seen something the day of Bunker Todd's murder? He was always out wandering around the town. What if he had seen the murderer?

"Rex Perskie," she said suddenly.

"Where?"

"No, I mean he's back in town. Maybe he's the one who's after Freddy."

"For what?"

"Rex could be the one who killed Bunker Todd. I saw them talking the day he died. Freddy could be a witness."

"Anything's possible."

"Or the convenience store murderer could be following him. If Freddy knows about the guns."

"I wouldn't worry too much about that one. The sort of criminal mastermind who likes to tie up loose ends doesn't usually rob Seven-Elevens. When we find the Seven-Eleven killer, he's gonna turn out to be some wacked-out crack addict who doesn't even know Freddy exists. The murder weapon is just something he picked up on the black market."

"You don't suppose the poor kid is imagining the whole business of being followed, do you? I've thought for years he needed psychological help."

"Maybe he noticed me following him," Dave said.

"You? When?"

"This morning."

"Couldn't have been you, then. He told Saraleigh about it days ago." She salted four pretzels and put them in the toaster oven to be ready for the next rush. "Come to think of it, he told her about it before the murder."

"The Seven-Eleven Murder?"

"No. Bunker Todd's murder."

"Which you think was committed by Rex," he said.

"I don't know what I think. What do you think? What should we do?"

"Keep an eye out, and see what develops."

"You aren't using Freddy for bait, are you?"

"Oh, no, no. Wouldn't think of it."

"Because if anything happens to that boy—"

"He'll be okay, Vinnie." He opened the freezer lid and began to sort the frozen food, ice cream and Popsicles on one side, pretzels and pizza on the other. "I like it better when things are neatly sorted," he said. "What you need, you know, is a kid of your own."

"Really."

"Sugary junk food on one side, salty fatty junk food on the other. You and Mac Barrow. Is there something going on there?"

"Going on?"

"You seem to have so much in common. Bach to Bach, ballet to ballet, all that good stuff."

"What's it to you, Dave?"

"I'd feel more comfortable if you were settled."

"I am settled."

"I mean if you . . ."

"If I had a man?"

"I guess so. It's like, then I could stop thinking about you."

"You don't have to stop thinking about me. It depends on what you think."

He took his head out of the freezer case. "You know what I think."

Again the eyes. If only she could remember not to look at them. "I think about you too sometimes," she said.

He turned back to the freezer. Having shifted all the Bomb Pops and Italian ices to the right-hand side of the case, he began to gather the bags of frozen pretzels in his arms.

Just when his hands were completely full, the phone in his breast pocket rang. "Get that for me, will you?" he said.

Mother Grey plucked it out and said hello. An almost-familiar voice, teetering between a boy's treble and a man's basso, said, "Is my father there? This is Rick Dogg." Ricky. Of course. She hadn't seen him in a year, not since they all went to the Trenton Thunder game and he made himself sick on the refreshments. The boy was getting very tall even then.

She gave the phone to Dave.

"What's up?" he said. There was a pause, and then he said, "Right. I'll be there in a couple of minutes." He hung up.

"Is something the matter?" Mother Grey asked.

"Felicia is . . . she's over at the neighbor's, and they can't get her to leave, he says."

"What in the world?"

"She's drinking again, Vinnie."

"Oh."

"You can handle this now, right?" he said, indicating the shack and its components.

"Certainly."

"See you." She watched him go, all the way to the parking lot. Behind one of the cars Schwartz stood talking earnestly with someone whose blue spikes stuck up; through the glass she almost thought she saw Schwartz give this person money and take a package from him.

11

They were still trying to reach Horace Burkhardt's daughter Allison. Horace hadn't been able to remember the name of the hotel where she had gone for her vacation, or even the name of the city. It was either Cancún or Tijuana, or maybe Acapulco, he said, he wasn't sure.

For her part, Mother Grey couldn't remember his daughter's last name. Hadn't she been married to one of the de Leos? No, that was Delight van Buskirk's grandniece. Mother Grey had accepted the chore of caring for Allison's Great Dane as long as Horace was in the hospital, and she was beginning to feel nervous. Sparky was a good-tempered dog, but he was still a puppy, and he was huge.

He was crying and carrying on so, all by himself in Horace's house, that Mother Grey let him into the rectory on Thursday night when the rest of her string quartet came over. Dr. Sheila made a fuss over him and scratched his ears, but Walter and Kenneth eyed him nervously, as though they expected him to try to cut his milk teeth on their instruments. Mother Grey finally put him in the kitchen with Towser, hoping the two of them could manage to get along.

Her musician friends had abandoned their old custom of having dinner before playing, partly because of Mother Grey's cooking, she suspected, although the others were too polite to say so. Instead of trying to feed them a whole meal, she fixed them a little dessert, Entenmann's low-fat crumb cake and a pot of good coffee. The cake went onto the new bread and butter plates, and the coffee went into the new cups. She carried it all out to the coffee table.

She found them gossiping about Bunker Todd's murder.

"So, Vinnie, you found another body," said Sheila.

"I did not. I did not find another body. I found a golf cart turned over in the canal. I do not make a habit of finding bodies."

"At least my house is safe now from Bunker Todd's convention-hotel project," Sheila said.

"Interesting," said Walter. "Tell me, where were you and Jake yesterday afternoon?"

"At work," said Sheila. "With witnesses. Both of us. Ironclad alibis."

"What I want to know is, what was this guy doing tooling around the bike path on a golf cart?" Kenneth said.

"He did it all the time," Sheila said. "Ever since he broke his leg. He already had a golf cart, and he used that instead of getting a motorized wheelchair. I used to see him go by often."

"Doesn't seem like it would be safe," Kenneth said.

Sheila said, "I guess it was safe enough until somebody shot him."

"Do you know how he came to break his leg?" Mother Grey asked.

"No," said Sheila. "I thought he fell over the state's construction equipment, the way he said he did. Is there some question?"

"The coaches all had funny looks when they were talking about it at the hearing, if you remember, and they wouldn't tell me what was on their minds. I thought you might have heard something."

But this time the finger on the pulse of Fishersville failed to feel a throb. "Nope," said Sheila.

The coffee was strong, the cake agreeably sugary. They dusted themselves off and tuned up. Scarcely had they begun to play when a telephone call came from Horace.

"They're letting me out of this joint tomorrow morning at nine, Mother Vinnie. Can you come and pick me up?"

And so on Friday morning after she ate breakfast and walked both the dogs, she drove right over to the medical center to get him.

The nurse at the desk said Horace was nearly ready to leave. She showed Mother Grey where his room was, right down the hall. He was sitting in the chair beside the empty bed, the valise that Mother

Grey had packed for him the day before waiting at his feet.

"How are you, Horace?" she said.

"The doctor wants to talk to me one more time before they let me out of this joint," he told her. "But they say I'm all right. Did anyone get in touch with my daughter?"

"Not yet," she said.

"I remember now where it is that she went," he said. "It was the Yucatán Peninsula."

"When do you expect her back?"

"Saturday."

"That's tomorrow," Mother Grey said. "We might just as well wait until she gets here."

A doctor came in with pen and clipboard. "We're going to let you go home, Mr. Burkhardt," he said. "But you should have someone looking after you. And of course you shouldn't be driving."

"Right now, you mean."

"No, sir, I mean at all. If you have one of these spells behind the wheel of a car, you might kill somebody."

"I have to get to St. Augustine," said Horace. "My girlfriend is down there."

The doctor laughed; he was still young; he didn't understand. "Take the train, Mr. Burkhardt," he said. "Take a plane."

"What about my motor home?"

"You can hire somebody to drive it."

"Nobody drives my motor home but me."

"Well, take it or leave it, Mr. Burkhardt, you can't drive anymore."

After hearing this sentence, Horace sulked all the way back to Fishersville. He was so low in his spirits that Mother Grey invited him to come to dinner that night to cheer him up.

The meal came out of cans, but she fancied it up a little by mixing it into a casserole, something she had learned when she was in Girl Scouts—the last time she had taken an interest in cooking.

She stirred mushroom soup into tuna fish, sprinkled crushed potato chips over the top, and popped the casserole into the carefully preheated oven.

A light rain was falling; it made a pleasant patter on the roof. While the meal cooked—was it thirty minutes at 350 degrees, or fifty minutes at 330 degrees? No matter, when it smelled good she would take it out—Mother Grey curled up in the flowered chair to peruse the latest vestment catalog from Almy. It would be nice to have a new stole for Sunday services. This one with the birds on it was lovely. Too bad about the price.

Horace arrived bearing dessert, a half-eaten bag of cookies. Physically he seemed to have recovered almost completely from his attack, whatever it was, but mentally he was more despondent than ever. She clasped his hands in welcome and ushered him in.

"Thanks for asking me," he said. "Nobody else will speak to me. Did you know nobody talks to me anymore? Lived too damned long."

"Oh, Horace, stop that," said Mother Grey.

She put him at the place across from hers at the old oak dining table. After a short prayer she produced the casserole, along with a few little lettuce leaves that passed for salad. The food was tasty, and the new flowered dishes very satisfactory indeed.

But as they ate, Horace continued to complain of still being alive until finally Mother Grey said, "You seem depressed, Horace. Have you talked to a doctor about it? Sometimes that can help."

"Doesn't seem any point in talking to doctors; I've lived too damned long already."

All right, that's enough, let's confront this head-on. "Horace, are you having thoughts of killing yourself?"

The old man put down his fork and considered the question. "Sometimes I think if I wanted to kill myself, I could just put a gun to my chest, and it would be all over," he said. " 'Course I don't have a gun, so there's no point in that, is there?"

The casserole was sawdust in her mouth. She was going to have to do suicide counseling again. "If you killed yourself, Horace, the people who love you would be devastated. Your daughter would never get over it. I want you to think about that." So he had a plan—shooting himself in the chest. It was always more dangerous when they had a plan. Fortunately it involved a handgun, which, as he said, he didn't have.

Horace gave her a blank stare, as though trying to remember what they had been discussing.

"Doesn't it cheer you up to know you won't have to sell the ball field?" she said.

"Doesn't matter anymore," he said. "Now I know who my real friends are. Damned few of them."

And the ones he had, he couldn't remember their names.

"Have you heard from your daughter?" Mother Grey asked him. It was definitely time to get him some help.

"She isn't coming back. I got a postcard from her. I think she's going to marry a Mexican and stay there."

A light tap on the front door caused Towser to bark and carry on. She opened to admit Detective Cranmer from the county prosecutor's office. The call was probably not social; under his wrinkled raincoat Cranmer was wearing a coat and tie, which no man would do in summer in Fishersville if it weren't professionally necessary.

"I'm not interrupting your dinner, am I?" he said.

"We were just about finished," Mother Grey said. "Come in, you can have coffee with us."

"Ah. Mr. Burkhardt."

"Don't believe I've had the pleasure," the old man said.

"This is Detective Cranmer, Horace," Mother Grey said.

Cranmer flashed his shield. "I need to clear up a few points about the murder. I'm glad you're here, sir. I'd like to talk to you too."

"Murder," Horace said. "Shame about that feller. What was his name?"

"Todd," said Mother Grey.

"Hanh?"

"Todd. Bunker Todd."

"Right. Bunker Todd. Too bad he's dead." This expression of regret sounded strange, coming from a man who had all but perished from joy on hearing the news of Todd's death. Was Horace a better actor than Mother Grey would have guessed? Probably not; probably he had forgotten the whole thing already.

"Mr. Burkhardt hasn't been well," she said. "He just came home from the hospital." She set out three matching cups and filled them with coffee. Bliss! If a fourth person came calling, she would still have one more cup.

"You were around town Wednesday morning, though, right?" said Cranmer. "Unless there are two Horace Burkhardts in Fishersville. See, I have you on my list here."

"List?" said Mother Grey.

"Of people who were seen on the canal bank Wednesday. So. What were you doing at the time of the murder, Mr. Burkhardt?"

Horace said, "Walking the dog."

"Mr. Burkhardt is taking care of his daughter's Great Dane this week," said Mother Grey. "That's him you hear woofing, over in the—"

"And where were you walking this dog?"

"In that park by the canal bank," he said. "I had him off the leash, and he was finally getting some exercise—big dogs need exercise, you know—when along came the ranger, so I hooked him back up and came home before he could get a chance to give us a hard time like he always does, the son of a bitch."

"Did you see anything suspicious?" Cranmer asked.

"Don't know what that would be."

"Guns lying around, bloodstains, people who looked guilty, anything out of the ordinary," Cranmer prompted.

"Nothing unusual at all."

"So, the park ranger," Cranmer said, making a note on his pad. "I'll have to talk to him too, since he was in the area."

"And what did you want to see to me about?" said Mother Grey.

"It says in your statement that you heard a report and a splash," Cranmer said. "I don't suppose you looked at your watch or anything."

"No. It was about ten-thirty, give or take five minutes. I can't be more precise than that."

"Too bad."

But she was thinking, there was something mysterious about Bunker Todd—"Have you heard how he broke his leg?" she said. "There's something strange about it. It might be important." Clearly the townspeople didn't believe his story, but they weren't saying what they thought had really happened.

"I thought he fell over some construction equipment on the bike trail," Cranmer said.

"Nope," the old man said, with a wise look. Ah! Horace knew the story!

"How, then?"

"It's not my story," said Horace.

"Let's hear it anyhow," Cranmer said.

Having a willing audience, Horace cheered up

some and began the long tale. "I was having breakfast in Delio's a couple of weeks ago," he said, "when this feller came in. He said he was one of Beetee's workmen, a roofing assistant. Did you know that miserable bastard hired all out-of-town people on that project? With men right here in Fishersville, perfectly competent workmen, needing jobs."

"A shame," said Mother Grey.

"This guy had just come from—what did they call it?—Fishersville Holdings. He's holding it, all right. That piece of land used to belong to my dead sister. Miserable bastard bought it off my niece for a song."

"Tsk," said Mother Grey, beginning to wonder where all this was leading. Cranmer was taking notes frantically, no doubt listing Horace's motives for killing the miserable bastard.

"So this guy sits down and tells us this story. He says he is nailing shingles to the roof of one of these piles in the so-called Fishersville Holdings when he sees two men and a woman come running out of one of the other houses. The first guy has his pants half off. The second guy chases him about a hundred yards and whacks the first guy across the leg with a baseball bat. Whack! Said he could hear it clear up on the rooftop. The woman runs away."

"Did the workman recognize any of these people?"

"Too far away. Next day here comes Bunker Todd with his leg in a cast and he's gonna sue the state. Everybody who heard the guy shooting his mouth off in Delio's knew what the real story was."

Naturally the jealous husband or father or whatever he was would have kept quiet; he could have been arrested for felonious assault. So when Todd claimed he had tripped over some construction equipment on the bike trail, there was nobody to give him the lie.

Except the man on the roof. If, indeed, the man on the roof was telling the truth.

"I'd like to talk to this guy," Cranmer said. "See what I think of his story. If he's not making the whole thing up, he might be able to tell us who broke Todd's leg, and that might be the guy who came back for a shot at the rest of him."

"Or maybe one of his women did it," Horace said.

"Women?" said Cranmer. "Multiple women?"

Mother Grey was thinking, who would happen to come along carrying a baseball bat in a housing development right next to the Little League ball field? Who else but one of the coaches? Of course, the Angels were not by any means the only team in the League, and there were plenty of coaches with attractive wives besides Tommy Hudson. So probably it wasn't even him.

"He had quite a reputation, this Bunker Todd," said Horace. "He used to have a nice wife, but he left her."

"Did you ever see the guy before?"

"Who?"

"This man who said he was on the roof. What did he look like?"

"I almost thought I knew him," said Horace. "Little short feller, long greasy hair, sort of mouse-blond. Tattoos on his arms."

"Did he have a devil's head on the back of his right hand?" Mother Grey asked.

"Yeah. You know him?"

Rex Perskie.

12

Ever since the rectory fire, Mother Grey had suffered a recurring dream from time to time featuring an abandoned house. Sometimes it began as she approached on foot, hiking through the woods. Other times she drove down a long driveway, little more than two dirt tracks the width of car wheels, and parked under a grove of trees. At first it was an attractive house, if somewhat the worse for wear; the proportions were pleasing; a front porch offered shade from the sun, a place to rest. Someone she knew was waiting for her to come inside.

Then as she drew closer, the house grew more and more sinister. The glass was broken out of all the windows. The front door hung half off the hinges. She went up the steps and saw that shotgun pellets had pitted the paint of the shingles, once a light gray-blue.

Unpleasantness, even menace, waited beyond the door.

˙But she had to go in.

She put her hand on the doorknob and pulled the heavy weathered door open, scraping it loudly along on the floor of the porch because the broken hinges wouldn't hold the door's weight. Inside it was dark. And it smelled—mold-smells, mouse-smells, and a wisp of smoke.

Smoke?

She lifted her head from the pillow, and the dream was forgotten as completely as the name of Horace's daughter's Mexican vacation spot.

Only the memory of the smoke smell remained. Ever since the old rectory burned, the smell of smoke frightened her on some deep irrational level; inside this sensible clergywoman beat the heart of a spooked horse. Skittishly she rose and sniffed all around the rectory but concluded that the smoke was only in her dream.

The feel of the thing followed her into the bathroom. Brushing her teeth, she could almost remember what it had been about. She rinsed out and spit, took a swig of the blue stuff that was saving her from expensive dental work in the absence of fluoride in the Fishersville water, and spit again.

Today was Saturday. All her chores were done except the sermon, and that would come to her this evening as she ate her solitary supper—canned chili again, and how she looked forward to it. The whole day stretched before her, a good ten hours in which to find the killer of Bunker Todd. Not counting time to see Freddy's play-off game, of course.

Because she had decided in her sleep, somewhere deep in the dream she could not remember, that she herself had to find and capture the murderer of Bunker Todd.

Horace had said Todd had an estranged wife someplace. If he was such a great womanizer, maybe she knew something about his women. *Cherchez la femme* and all that. Doylestown. They said he came from Doylestown.

The Pennsylvania phone book in the dust under her bed was a couple of years old. It showed a Doylestown telephone listing for Bunker Todd. When she called the number, a woman answered and identified herself as Linda Todd.

"Mrs. Todd, I'm Mother Lavinia Grey of St. Bede's in Fishersville."

"I already have a church affiliation, but thank you very much for calling."

"I'm not calling about that. I have some questions about your husband's death I was hoping you could help me with."

"Questions about Bunker's death? I've already talked to the police."

"Please. I'd very much like to come and see you."

"Bunker's funeral is this afternoon. If I'm to talk to you, it will have to be this morning. Can you be here in half an hour?"

"I think so."

"Good. I'll see you then." She gave directions to her house; they seemed simple enough.

Hoping to inspire confidence, trust, and a willingness to open up, Mother Grey put on the clerical collar. On her way out to the car, she found Horace Burkhardt skulking on the back doorstep.

"Why, Horace. Good morning."

"Mother Vinnie, I need a favor," he said. "Can you drive the motor home as far as the interstate? You could put your bicycle inside it and ride back to town from there. It would mean a lot to me."

"Not right now," she said. "What's this all about?"

"I need a lift out of town," said Horace. "Jack Kreevitch won't let me drive. Says he'll arrest me if he catches me driving. I have to get to Florida. He's trying to keep me away from his mother, bless her."

"You sure it isn't that he heard what the doctor said about you and driving?"

"That's a load of crap, Mother Vinnie. I can drive as well as I ever could. Come on. What do you say?"

"I can't do it right now, really, Horace," Mother Grey said. "I'm late for an appointment. Can it wait?"

"I have to get out of town *right now*," he said.

"I'll be back in an hour or two," she said. "We'll talk about it then."

"Talk," he muttered as she got in the car. Taking Horace to the interstate and setting him on a course for Florida didn't seem to Mother Grey to be a good idea. What if he should have one of his seizures, as the doctor predicted? He could be a danger to others as well as himself.

And what did he plan to do with his daughter's dog?

Allison would be back today, or tomorrow anyway, if, as Mother Grey hoped, Horace had misunderstood her postcard about marrying the Mexican. When Allison got back, she would talk him out of this scheme somehow.

Linda Todd lived in a stone farmhouse outside of Doylestown. Mother Grey found her working in her garden, a magazine-quality garden in the English style, with borders of foxgloves and delphiniums and a flagstone path with thyme growing out of the cracks. "My word," Mother Grey breathed. Gardening was the skill whose effects she most admired, and whose exertions she least practiced, after cooking.

Freckled, wrinkled, her straw-colored hair streaked with white, Linda Todd might have spent her entire life digging in this sunny yard. She stood up, brushed the dirt off her knees, and invited Mother Grey into her cool and shady house. A pitcher of iced tea and some cookies waited on the kitchen table.

"You wanted to talk about my husband."

"I'm looking into his death," Mother Grey said. "I thought maybe you knew who his associates were after he left you."

"Actually he didn't leave me. I asked him to go," she said. "We are still—we were still married at the time of his death. We never divorced." There was an edge to her voice, as though this point was very important to her.

"Do you mind if I ask why you wanted him to leave?" said Mother Grey, thinking, *Maybe she'll tell me the name of the woman, or the names of the women.*

"I've never told this to anyone."

"Whatever you tell me will be entirely confidential."

She put down her iced tea and stared at her hands. "He would only bathe once a week."

"Oh."

"He never brushed his teeth before going to bed." Mother Grey glanced around the fastidious kitchen, which was as far inside the house as Linda Todd was willing go with gardening mud on her shoes, and began to understand. Mrs. Todd went on; she was tired of picking up his laundry, she said. The maid came only once a week, and all the rest of the time she had to deal with Bunker's smelly underwear and socks. He left them everywhere, and their son did too, when he was home, following Bunker's horrible example. "It's embarrassing to admit," she said, massaging her forehead. "One day I woke up and couldn't stand the smell of him anymore."

"I see," said Mother Grey, and the memory came to her unbidden of how nice Dave Dogg smelled, even when he needed a shower. It must have something to do with pheromones. Clearly the Todds were not meant to be together.

"Are you married, Mother Grey? Priests in the Episcopal Church can marry, can't they?"

"They can, but I'm not married. My first—my husband died many years ago, before I was called to the priesthood."

"Sad. But do you know, I can't grieve for Bunker. I know it will hit me one of these days that he's gone."

"You have children?"

"Two. Jean has a job in the city, and Randolph is still in college."

"What about you? Do you work outside the home?" Mother Grey asked.

"I spend my time in church, gardening, volunteering at the hospital, doing things with the women's club. It's a satisfying life." She was clasping and unclasping her freckled hands, feeling her fingers, playing with her rings.

"The women's club," Mother Grey murmured. It seemed so archaic.

"That sort of lifestyle is still available to those who like it and who have the time. Not everybody embraces yuppie values, not even these days. But of course you know that, Mother Grey. I was forgetting." She nibbled a cookie. "You know, you remind me a lot of my Jean, although her life is very different from yours. She isn't married either."

"Speaking of women," said Mother Grey. "Were there other women in your husband's life, that you knew of?"

"Oh, yes," she said. "There were women. I used to smell them on him."

"Their perfume."

"No, other things."

Mother Grey looked out the window at the perfect garden. The tall spikes of foxglove moved gently back and forth in the freshening breeze.

* * *

The same wind was beginning to stir the purple loosestrife along the canal bank where Jack Kreevitch pedaled his beat. As he cruised behind the Acme, he suddenly came upon the ranger car parked in the middle of the trail. Or not even parked. It was stopped, the driver-side door open, the engine running, the emergency brake engaged. George Pitts, the ranger, seemed to be nowhere around.

"Hey, Pitts!" Kreevitch called, but there was no answer. His voice echoed off the brick walls of the old umbrella factory on the other side of the canal. *I'll save the state some gas, anyway,* he thought, and he turned off the ignition and put the key in his pocket. No use leaving this here for the kids to drive the car into the canal. "Yo! Pitts!"

But George Pitts in his brown ranger uniform was neither to be seen nor heard.

Kreevitch poked around in the bushes, went up the trail and back a little way. No Pitts. Could he have gone through the bushes to the Acme to pick up a cold drink? It seemed unlikely that he would have left the car running. Pitts was a stickler for rules.

Kreevitch pushed his bike through the break in the shrubbery and scrambled down the bank to the Acme parking lot.

Trays of blazing annuals lined the sidewalk in front of the Acme, red, yellow, and brilliant orange in the noonday sun. Freddy Kane and Garrett Hudson, in their Angels uniforms complete with cleats, had set up a small table by the door to sell candy for the Fishersville Youth Baseball League. Sweat trickled down under their caps. "Buy some candy, Uncle Jack?" said Garrett.

"Got all I need at home," Kreevitch said. "Brian and Chris are selling it. Aren't you two supposed to be over at the field?"

"Oh, yeah," said Freddy. "Guess we better pack it up, Garrett."

"Listen. Have you guys seen Mr. Pitts, the ranger? He would have been wearing a tan uniform."

"No, sir," said Freddy. But boys don't always pay attention to what happens around them, so he went inside to check with the Acme clerks.

The cold blast of air conditioning that met his sweaty body was almost paralyzing. None of the clerks had seen the ranger. Kreevitch bought a cold bottle of soda and went back to the ranger car.

Maybe Pitts had fallen into the canal. Kreevitch saw no unusual disturbance on the canal bank. Still, the water was so muddy that fifty or sixty guys could be lying down there and never be seen.

Maybe it was time to call for backup and seal off the area with yellow tape. Again.

The drawer was sticking again in Rochelle Hudson's telephone desk, the one Tommy had built for her five years ago, the one whose drawer had never worked right. She liked the color she had painted it, and she liked the spring flower decoupage she had done, following the directions in an article in *Family Circle* on decorating like the rich. It was a pretty little table. Until you tried to open the drawer.

Yesterday, she recalled, the drawer had stuck because of something heavy in it, and when she finally pried the damned thing open, there sat this gun. It would have been alarming if she weren't so worried about Dawn, but as it was, she merely mentioned it to Tommy, and he grunted, like she wasn't supposed to talk about it, and so she let it alone.

But today the gun wasn't there anymore. Something else was making the drawer stick. Incompetent workmanship was Rochelle's guess. Finally she got the thing pried open, straightened it out in its tracks again, and wrenched her address book out of it before she jammed it closed.

Bunker Todd's old number was in the book, from before he left his wife. Hopefully the woman hadn't had it changed. Linda Todd answered after the third ring.

"It's Rochelle Hudson, Mrs. Todd. I'm calling about the Riverside Hiltshire project. It was terribly important to Bunker—to Mr. Todd—and I just know you'll want to go ahead with it, as the new majority stockholder in Beetee Associates—"

"I'm sorry, Miss—what did you say your name was? Nothing could be further from my mind right now than Mr. Todd's terribly important projects."

"But I'm sure you'll want to think about it very soon. I realize it's early for me to be contacting you—"

"You could say that. I'll be leaving for Mr. Todd's funeral in five minutes."

"Still, you should consider the enormous rate of return that this project would yield," Rochelle went

on. "For what is really quite a small initial invest-
ment. The potential for growth in this area is tremendous. And the tax benefits—"

"You'll have to excuse me," Mrs. Todd said. "But I
can assure you that I have no interest in developing a
resort hotel in Fishersville."

"Take some more time to think it over," Rochelle
Hudson said. "Please." *Maybe if I beg.* "I can call you
again on Monday, when you've had more—"

"No, my dear," Linda Todd said. "My husband
was the driving force behind Beetee Associates, and
now that he's gone, I have no desire to pursue his
plans."

"Is it the Little League?" Rochelle asked. "Because if that's it, we can always—"

"No, I haven't any particularly warm feelings for
baseball," Linda Todd said. "But neither do I want to
put up a hotel in Fishersville. I'm sorry. Better luck
with your next project."

Rochelle hung up. The deal for the hotel was as
dead as Bunker Todd.

Lost was her big score, her ticket out of Fishersville, her huge commission. She glanced around at
the peeling wallpaper, the stuffing coming out of the
couch, the pile of decorating magazines in the corner. The magazines were full of cheery handicraft
projects. Over the years she had tried them, each
more time-consuming and ineffectual than the last,
until finally she took a hard look at her house, piled
with painted flower pots, crocheted tissue holders,
and ditzy pillows, and realized that what was re-
quired here was nothing but money.

Not that money was uppermost in her mind right now. She was worried sick about her daughter. All night long she had scarcely closed an eye, and when she did drop off, it was to some nightmare about Dawn being dragged into the bushes and killed, or carried away screaming in the back of a van, maybe to the city. You read all kinds of things in the papers.

Dawn had been such a beautiful baby. Rochelle remembered playing with her little fingers, her incredibly tiny nails, after she was born. Every time the nurses brought her in wrapped up like a peanut, Rochelle unwrapped her again to make sure she was still all there.

And now where was she? Rochelle had called all of Dawn's girlfriends twice, and all they would tell her was that she didn't understand Dawn. "No, really. I don't know where she is," they said, knowing she thought they were lying. "But she isn't like you think. You don't really understand the sort of person Dawn is, Mrs. Hudson." Rochelle had no idea what these girls were talking about.

"She isn't like you think," they said. What did they think she thought? What, for that matter, did they know of what Dawn was really like? They didn't know what she was really like. At that age, untested by life, they didn't know what they themselves were really like.

She called the police station again. Still no news.

In the bottom drawer of the desk she found fifty wallet-size copies of a recent likeness of Dawn. Tommy had ordered them the other time she ran away, but before he had a chance to give them out, she had come back. There was typing paper there too. She took a couple of sheets.

Then she sat down at the kitchen table and began to design a flyer. They would get it printed and circulate it everywhere in the country, Canada and Mexico even, post it in all the police stations and Laundromats. MISSING. HAVE YOU SEEN THIS CHILD?

She started to cry. Maybe a little drink would take the edge off. Just one. The whiskey bottle was still under the sink.

In fifteen minutes Garrett's game would be starting. Rochelle had chores to do as the Angels' team mother, candy money to collect, bookkeeping to take care of for the team. On the other hand, it wasn't as though these were ordinary times. Under certain circumstances you needed a little something just to get through the day.

As she gulped down a fruit-juice glass half full of whiskey, the back door rattled.

Dawn walked in.

"Where have you been?"

"At a friend's house."

"Where in the world have you been? Your father and I were worried sick about you!"

"You didn't have to worry. I can take care of myself. Listen, Mom, I need a hundred dollars."

"What for?"

"My share of the rent."

"What rent?"

"A bunch of us are going down the shore for the summer."

"The hell you are."

"Mom, it's okay. I can go."

"No, you can't."

"Well, I'm going. My friends are going, and I'm going. You don't want me around here anyhow. All we do is fight."

"What friends?"

"My girlfriends. Lisa, Joanne, Patty. Randy."

"These people are all too old for you. And Randy is a boy. What are you thinking of!"

"What's the difference? What do you care? You don't care what happens to me. Anyway, you're never home. You're always out doing some real estate deal."

"I don't think that's fair. Somebody has to put food on the table, since your father was laid off."

"*Or* some real estate *dealer*."

"Watch your mouth."

"Mom, I'm very mature for my age. Lots of girls my age are married or living alone in apartments."

"I don't think so. In Appalachia, maybe, where they all marry their first cousins. Or the city, where the mothers are drug addicts. But you have a perfectly good home here, your father and I love you."

"Randy and I want to get married."

"Oh, my God. Baby, you're fourteen."

"I have to get out of this house. Why won't you give me money?"

"I don't understand what you want. Why would you want to leave home? Stay and finish your education. At least get through high school, for heaven's sake. Then if you and Randy still want to get married—"

"Mom, I need the money. They're waiting for it. It's my share."

"No."

"Give it to me."

"Honey, this is not like giving you permission to go on a class trip."

She sighed. "All right, I guess I'll have to tell you. I'm expecting his child."

"You're what!"

"I'm pregnant. The baby is due in January. You're going to be a grandmother."

"You're too young to get married, you're too young to be a mother, you're too young to have sex, for God's sake. What were you thinking of?"

"Freedom," she said, tossing her hair. It was red again, Rochelle noticed.

"Some freedom with a baby. Have you any idea—? No, I guess not. Well, let me tell you. Having a baby is a jail sentence. It's like twenty years in prison. I could have had a career as a model if I hadn't had you. I had a future."

"I *know* what I want to do with my *life*."

"This is going to kill your father."

"If he hasn't already died from the way you carry on, I don't think it will."

So Rochelle slapped her.

This time she hit back. But Rochelle was still bigger. They grappled; Dawn pulled Rochelle's hair and tried to bite her. Rochelle dragged her daughter down the hall, flung her in her room, locked the door, and pocketed the key.

Her face was horrifying when she straightened her hair in the hall mirror, the face of a mad stranger. *What am I doing?* she thought. *What have I done?*

She shouted through the door: "I have to go to your brother's baseball game. Try to get hold of yourself. We'll talk about this with your father as soon as the game is over."

The Angels were "versing" the Mariners, as Freddy put it, with glory and big trophies at stake. Everyone in town who cared about youth baseball was in the bleachers, a surprisingly large number of people. Schwartz and Danny had come to root for Freddy. The Reeker boys were there too, sitting on the first tier. Howie's tall blue spikes almost obstructed Mother Grey's view.

She had found a good seat early, where the shadow of one of the trees would fall across her face and shield her eyes in case the sun came out again. She was basted in Skin-So-Soft. Clipped to her hair was a bow made out of a dryer sheet she had begged from Marla.

She had come to the game not only to watch Freddy but to watch out for him, since Dave wasn't in Fishersville today. She had also come to beam with pleasure on Mac Barrow. He had gotten the Hook and Hastings tracker organ at St. Bede's up and running at last, after a fashion, and all they needed now was a choir, after which the wealthy parishioners would come. And face it, his buns were cute.

Coaches from other teams were in the bleachers behind her, discussing the precarious situation of the ball field. "I think the city ought to buy it," one of them said.

"We should have bought it before. We should have got a ninety-nine-year lease before we built these dugouts and the shack."

"C'mon, man. Horace is eighty-four. He ain't gonna live another ninety-nine years."

"Well, okay. The city ought to buy it off him."

The boy on the loudspeaker announced the starting lineup. The Angels were considered the visiting team today—all the teams in the league were from Fishersville—and so they were first at bat. Freddy was fifth up.

Saraleigh, squeezed in beside Mother Grey with the baby on her lap, fanned herself with her hat. "I almost wish the rain would come," she said. "It's so stinkin' hot." The first Angel stepped up to the plate, shouldered his bat, and glared at the Mariner pitcher.

"Bre-e-ent, Bre-e-ent," the outfielders bleated. Whack! The little batter socked it a good one. When the dust cleared, he was on first base.

Next up was a tubby kid like a tiny Babe Ruth, who whacked the ball up, up, and a long way into the outfield. The Mariner's right fielder got underneath it, and it dropped softly into his glove for the Angels' first out.

The third batter was a girl, one of two on the team. "Where are the rest of the girls?" Mother Grey wanted to know. "Don't they like to play baseball?"

"These boys can be rough," Saraleigh said. "Most of the girls who used to play tee-ball with Freddy have joined the girls' softball league."

"Or quit," Marla said.

Rough? It was true that the Angels were aggressive about base stealing. By the time Freddy was up, the first batter had slid into third base in a cloud of dirt and was threatening to steal home. Trembling with compressed energy, he would inch farther and farther off third, awaiting his chance. More than once, the Mariners' catcher had to rip off his mask and rush to the plate to keep it covered.

The third time, he went too far, and the catcher nailed him. Two outs for the Angels.

Then pitcher Brent walked the girl, after which a tall slim boy stepped up to the plate and knocked a base hit.

Next up was Freddy. Saraleigh screamed herself hoarse. Three balls, two strikes, and then he hit the ball into left field and ran to first. The left fielder threw the ball to third as the spectators went wild. Mother Grey was on her feet, cheering.

The girl slid into third base as the ball plopped into the third baseman's glove. Tie goes to the runner. "Safe!" the umpire cried, doing that thing they do with their arms. Now three Angels were on base.

Garrett Hudson came up to bat.

Whiff.

"Strike!" bellowed the umpire.

"Boy, that would have gone right over the fence if he'd hit it," Saraleigh said.

"That's all right, Garrett! Take your time!" Rochelle hollered.

Garrett composed himself, waggled his arms, readjusted his stance, and held his bat up straight.

Whiff.

"Wait for it, Garrett!" Tommy Hudson shouted.

Then Garrett waited for it, and when at last it came, the count was two and two. Clong! Over the fence. The Angels came home one by one and at last Garrett, his face radiant with bliss as he rounded third base. This might be the greatest moment of his life.

Behind Mother Grey someone said, "Hi, babe." Saraleigh started violently. It was Rex Perskie. He had somehow materialized in the seat beside her while they were all cheering.

"Get lost, Rex," Saraleigh said.

"I gotta talk to you. It's important. Come with me where we can talk private."

"Take a hike. I ain't gonna talk to you, and I sure as hell ain't gonna go with you anyplace private."

"C'mon, babe, don't be that way. We have things between us we have to talk about. We're still family, right? I ain't gonna do nothin' bad to you. I just wanna talk. I have something to ask you. C'mon. For old times' sake."

"Listen, you stupid bastard, I'll tell you one last time. I got nothin' to say to you, and there ain't nothin' I want to hear you say to me."

"Well, shit on you then," he said, and climbed down out of the bleachers again.

Mother Grey did not notice which way he went, for the Angels made another thrilling play, so astonishing that it absorbed her complete attention. The little runner went from first to second, back to first again, and then back to second, as the umpire roared, the spectators moaned, and the coaches loudly argued points of baseball law. Mother Grey never did figure out what it was all about, but from the discussions she overheard, the spectacle involved the infield fly rule or some equally enigmatic dictum.

In the end he was called out. The Mariners came up to bat and failed to distinguish themselves. One inning gone, and the sky was growing darker. Mother Grey went to the shack and got herself a pretzel as the Mariners streamed out into the field to take up their positions.

Luckily there was a pretzel already cooked. The woman in the shack handed it to her and asked her whether she knew Rochelle Hudson.

"Yes, I do."

"Could you give her this message? Her daughter just called and left it." She gave Mother Grey a folded paper and, as she did so, rolled her eyes, as though to say, "The waywardness of daughters." But Mother Grey did not peek at the paper on her way back to the bleachers. She almost did, but she felt that it would have been rude.

The Angels were having no better luck this inning than the Mariners had. Coach seemed to have changed the lineup. Garrett was up again, with two outs showing on the scoreboard. As she screamed for Garrett to get a hit, Rochelle took the note absently from Mother Grey's fingers. But Garrett knocked two foul balls and then struck out.

The sky was now the color of roofing slate. Once again it was the Mariners' turn to bat, the Angels' turn in the field. Festooned with catcher gear, Freddy staggered to his place behind home plate.

The branches of the trees Mother Grey was sitting under began to lash in the rising wind; a few leaves and twigs tore loose and went flying away to the east. Marla Kreevitch made a dive for her red Angels hat and saved it just in time. Black clouds roiled overhead, in the distance a flash of lightning, then a crack of thunder. The little girls snuggled closer to Saraleigh.

"Think they'll call the game?" asked one of the coaches behind her.

"Nah," said the other one. "It'll blow over."

The first cold heavy drops of rain fell.

Garrett took his stand on the pitcher's mound, but something was missing. It was the strident cheering of Rochelle, no longer in her seat beside Marla. Mother Grey glanced around, but Rochelle was nowhere in sight. Freddy at least was in full view, squatting behind home plate with his glove up to receive the pitch.

And here it came. It wasn't one of Garrett's trickier pitches; the batter connected with it at once and drove it deep into center field.

The Angels made a number of disconcerting errors then. The rain was falling hard now; the ball must have gotten wet. You would have thought it was greased. By the time the Angels got control of it, the Mariner batter was rounding third and heading at top speed for home plate.

The shortstop threw to home, the catcher ripped off his mask in order to better see the ball and cover the base, and Mother Grey realized that the boy in the catcher's mask was not Freddy.

The Mariners scored. Thunder cracked. The coaches called their teams into the dugouts to wait out the storm. Down out of the bleachers climbed the spectators to stand in the doubtful shelter of the leafy trees. Of course Freddy had been in the dugout all the time. Hadn't he? Coach Hudson must be giving the other little fellow a chance to catch.

Mother Grey ran and ducked under the slight overhang of the shack roof; as long as the wind kept up from the same direction, she could stay dry there. She craned her neck to see into the Angels' dugout, but in their uniforms all the players looked alike to her.

Taking a deep breath, she made a mad dash through the mud and the cold pelting rain, past the opening in the chain-link fence to the dugout.

The players sat all in a row, soaking wet, hugging themselves and shivering. Their nylon uniforms were very thin. "Where's Freddy Kane?" she asked them.

"Freddy ain't here," they told her. Jack Kreevitch wasn't there either; he was still at work, patrolling the town in his official capacity. Mac Barrow was in charge.

She tried another tack: "Where's Tommy?"

"He was here a minute ago," Mac said. "I guess he's in the john."

"Are they going to call the game?" she said.

"No," said Mac. "It'll blow over." As he spoke, the hair stood up on all their heads, and there was a blinding flash and a tremendous clap of thunder.

13

Jack Kreevitch found George Pitts's body almost immediately. It was in the bushes and not in the water, so at least they didn't have to drag the canal for him.

Shot in the head. Right here in Fishersville. *God damn*, he thought, *this town is getting really dangerous*. If George Pitts could get himself shot in the middle of a Saturday afternoon, no one in town was safe. Kreevitch himself wasn't safe. He looked around, but he didn't see anyone.

Clumsy hunters? Snipers? Kids? One man shot in the head on the canal bank might have been a tragic coincidence, but two in the same week . . .

He radioed headquarters. More work for the county prosecutor's office.

Trying not to disturb the crime scene, Kreevitch looked around for clues. But the integrity of the crime scene was a joke; the rain was coming down in torrents now, obliterating everything. If there ever was a clue to be found, it would be gone, washed into the canal, by the time the county homicide people got there.

Scarcely had he formed this thought than Detective Cranmer and the county people arrived on the scene, all business, and took over.

The cold feeling running down Mother Grey's spine was only partly rain. Freddy was in some kind of danger, she was certain of it. "I have to find Freddy Kane right away," she said to the boys. "Can't you tell me which way he went?"

"Oh, yeah," said one boy. "I forgot to tell you. This guy came around and said something bad to Freddy, and then Coach took the guy behind the dugout."

"What guy?" she said.

"I think it was his old stepfather."

"Rex Perskie?"

"Right."

"Did either of them come back after that?" Mother Grey said. The wind was screaming, the rainwater falling almost sideways.

"What?" said the boy.

"Did they come back?"

"No," the boy said.

With a crack, boom! a huge limb ripped loose from the tree Mother Grey had been sitting under earlier, partly crushing the bleachers. Luckily most of the spectators had made a run for their cars ten minutes before that, and the rest, including

Saraleigh and the girls, were huddled on the other side of the tree. The coach came over from the Mariners' dugout. "I guess we'll call the game," he said. "Hate to do it. What do you think?"

"Right," Mac Barrow said. "Let's call the game." His voice could scarcely be heard over the howling wind. Then along came Jack Kreevitch on his bicycle, soaked clear through, water and hair streaming into his face from under the bike helmet.

"You guys ready to play ball?" he said.

Mac and the other coach exchanged glances. "We kind of thought we'd call it off," Mac said.

"Hate to do it," said the other coach.

"Gonna send the little guys home then, are you?" Jack said.

"Yup."

"Okay, little guys. See you tomorrow. Batting practice is at one o'clock, okay?" The little guys all hollered, some with joy, others with disappointment. They threw their hats around and proceeded to slog out into the mud to find their parents' cars.

Mother Grey wrung her hands. "Can someone help me look for Freddy?" she said.

"Freddy Kane?" said Kreevitch. "Where did he go?"

"Rex Perskie was here," she said. "Now we can't find Tommy or Freddy."

A green Chevy Lumina quietly rolled up beside the fence, windshield wipers clicking. Dave Dogg checking in.

Saraleigh appeared in the dugout, carrying the girls. "What do you mean, you can't find Freddy?"

Mother and babies all had the same wide-eyed, slack-jawed scowl, clearly a family thing. Family resemblances seemed mystical and enchanting to Mother Grey, even when they weren't particularly attractive. Perhaps it was because she had been an only child.

"He seems to have wandered off," said Mac.

Dave turned off his lights and his engine.

"Freddeeee!" Saraleigh bellowed. They all paused to listen, but there was no reply. Dave Dogg got out of the car.

Kreevitch spoke in a low voice to Mother Grey and Mac. "I don't want to alarm you," he said, "but another dead body was found on the canal bank."

"My word!"

"Somebody is making a habit of shooting people to death down there. Until we find out who that is and get him in custody, I'm starting to think it would be a good idea to keep people away from the bike path."

"Who was it this time?" Mac said.

"George Pitts. The ranger."

"Jeez," said Saraleigh.

"I would have been here, but I had to go to a funeral," Dave said. "Where's Freddy?"

"Nobody knows," said Mother Grey.

"So you lost him."

"Oh, come on, Dave, I did the best I could. I'm not a trained policewoman."

"Tell me something, Dave," Saraleigh said. "Were you watching my son officially?"

"From time to time, I guess, more or less," Dave said.

"What was it you were expecting to happen to him?"

"Nothing," Mac said.

"We thought—" Kreevitch said.

"I was worried about him being followed," said Mother Grey. "Dave thinks maybe—"

"Dave thinks what?" Saraleigh said.

"Freddy's hat was found at the scene of a burglary in town," Dave said. "He knows something about who has those guns, Saraleigh, and that means he knows something about two murders."

"What!!"

"Three, maybe," said Kreevitch. "George Pitts was killed this morning."

Dave grunted at this news, and his face grew even more serious.

Saraleigh said, "So where's my kid?"

"Freddy's not all that lost," Kreevitch said. "We'll find him. Dave, why don't you take Saraleigh and the babies home? As long as you've got a car. They're soaking wet. Maybe Freddy went home. Probably you'll find him there sitting in front of the TV."

"Want a ride, Saraleigh?" Dave said.

"Yeah. Yeah, you bet your ass I want a ride. Also I want to get you someplace where I can have a few choice words with you, Dave Dogg. What the fuck are you playing at? Why didn't you tell me about this frigging hat business?" Continuing in this vein, she went out through the gate with Dave, carrying both girls, and climbed into the backseat of his car. As

Dave got in, Mother Grey saw her grim face lit up for a moment by the dome light. Dave would have a difficult ride back to her house.

The rain was slacking off. People who had been crouching under trees and shed roofs drifted into the dugout to see what was going on.

"Freddy Kane is missing. We're forming a search party," said Mother Grey. Most of the people there knew him: Besides Kreevitch and Mac there were Schwartz, Danny, the Reeker brothers, Marla, the two coaches from the other teams, the woman behind the snack counter, and several others.

"Right, a search party," said Kreevitch. "But not back toward town along the canal bank, I think, since I just came from that way, and I didn't see anybody. What about those empty houses in Fishersville Holdings? Could he have gone over there?"

"It's possible. Maybe he ducked into one of them to get out of the storm," she said. What she really feared was that Rex had kidnapped Freddy, possibly to get Saraleigh's attention, but he could have taken him over there as easily as anywhere else.

"Before you go looking, I want you all to buddy up," Kreevitch said. "Everybody pick a partner. Don't anybody go wandering around alone. Some weird things have been happening. Holler if you find Freddy, or—or if you see anything of Tommy Hudson."

"Why Tommy?" said Mother Grey.

"No reason," said Kreevitch. "Maybe he can tell us something." *Coach took him behind the dugout.* There was no one behind the dugout now. But there was a stain on the ground, almost like blood, melting into the mud.

"If you see any guns or hear any shots or like that, I want you to get out of there right away, okay?" Kreevitch added. When they all murmured or grunted, some showing signs of apprehension, he said to them, "Let's go."

Off they went; it felt more like a posse than a search party. There was an odd bump under Schwartz's shirt that, if she hadn't known better, Mother Grey could have sworn was a gun. Chick Reeker was making chests and saying he didn't care how tough Rex Perskie was, he wasn't gonna take nothin' off him. The women were calling, "Freddy! Freddy!" while the boys and men searched the underbrush with narrowed eyes.

To reach the houses under construction, they had to cross a shallow creek, picking their way over slimy stepping-stones. Even as they crossed it, the watercourse grew deeper with runoff from the storm. Mac Barrow appointed himself Mother Grey's partner. He steadied her elbow with a firm hand. It was nice, but she was used to walking in the woods and could probably have gotten across faster without him. Last over were Danny and Schwartz. The water by then was up around their ankles.

Everyone fanned out, two by two. Cries of "Freddy!" echoed from the walls of the half-finished houses and trailed away into the woods. No Freddy appeared, but the sun came out. Steam rose from the puddles. Mother Grey and Mac poked in the ditch and looked in the mud by the creek for traces of his little cleats.

"Look at that," said Mother Grey. "Vandals have already broken a window on that place."

"Maybe vandals," said Mac. "Maybe trespassers. Looks like the window's been forced." Mud was smeared on the windowsill; there was a footprint, much bigger than Freddy's foot.

"Shall we?" she said.

"By all means." He shoved the window up, and they dragged their own wet muddy selves through the opening. Mac went first.

Inside, the track of the intruder showed clearly on the subflooring; he wore shoes with a deeply cut tread that trapped mud and then released it in square clumps. Temporary stairs went up to the second floor, less steep than a ladder but only just. The mudprints led up them. Mother Grey pushed ahead and went first, partly because she didn't want Mac Barrow to think she was a wimp and partly because she didn't want to think so herself.

She heard a sound behind the closet door at the top of the stairwell. Slowly, slowly she opened it, and there, crouched in the darkness, his mouse-blond hair tangled, his eyes red, was Rex Perskie. With one hand he held a bloody handkerchief to his nose, and with the other he held a pint bottle of Old Overholt to his lips.

"Hi, there, preacher lady," he said.

"What happened to your nose?" said Mother Grey.

"I had a little talk with Tommy Hudson."

"What have you done with Freddy?"

"What, are you looking for Freddy Kane? Tommy took him home."

Downstairs she heard the searchers coming in where Mac had unlocked the door, stamping the mud off their feet. Several of them came up the ladder, led by Jack Kreevitch. Others poked their heads up through the stairwell hole.

"Where's Freddy?" said Howie Reeker, swaggering boldly up to the closet door.

"Yeah, where'd you hide the body?" said Chick, right behind him.

Rex pulled himself laboriously to his feet and stood swaying. Even stiff drunk there was menace in him. The boys edged away.

"If I wanted to kill that little bastard, he'd have been dead a long time ago," Rex said. "Hiya, Jack. You looking for killers?"

"Just trespassers, I guess," Kreevitch said. "Mind showing me your hands, old buddy?"

"What's this shit?"

"Show me your hands."

"If you're looking for killers, you're looking in the wrong friggin' place."

"Show me your goddamned hands!" The crowd took a step backward. Rex performed an elaborate shrug, empty hands outspread.

"Now put them on top of your head."

"Oh, Kee-rist, Jack—"

"Now!"

He did as he was told, sullenly. "I got to tell you something," Rex said, as Kreevitch applied the handcuffs. "I saw Bunker Todd when he got his leg broke, and it wasn't by falling over no equipment."

"You have the right to remain silent," said Kreevitch.

"Fuck my right to remain silent."

"Shut up."

"You guys hear that? Did all of you hear that? Did you hear that too, little preacher lady? The official police don't want to hear my story of how Bunker Todd came to break his leg."

As Rex addressed the general throng, Kreevitch began to muscle him down the crude stairway. "How would you like me to break your mouth?" he muttered.

"Hear that? He's threatening a prisoner. And me in handcuffs. What's the charge, anyway? What am I being arrested for?"

"Trespassing. You have the right to remain silent, bro. I strongly suggest you use it."

"Oh, right. Then I get shot trying to escape before I can tell people how Bunker Todd—Ow! Take it easy!—broke his leg. Bunker Todd broke his leg—Ow!—by Tommy Hudson (that's your brother-in-law, ain't it, Jack?) hitting him with a baseball bat—Ow! Easy there!—when he found him in bed with Rochelle—Shit!!" Somehow Jack Kreevitch lost control of his prisoner, who fell the rest of the way down the stairs.

14

Officer Jack Kreevitch did not frog-march Rex Perskie all the way back into town, as Mother Grey half-feared, nor did he tie him behind his bicycle and drag him. One of the town police cars, summoned by Kreevitch, arrived on the scene, and they loaded Perskie into the back.

Still no Freddy. Rex Perskie had said Tommy Hudson took him home. If so, Dave Dogg and Saraleigh would have found him there.

"Want a ride?" Mac Barrow said. She did; it was getting almost chilly, and she was soaking wet. "Come on, put your bike in the trunk."

Here was another fancy feature of Sheila's bicycle. You could flip a lever and undo a nut, and the front wheel would come all the way off, enabling you to store the whole thing in the trunk of a BMW.

Inside, Mac's car smelled partly of new car and partly of cedar, although there were no tacky little deodorizing pine trees, at least not where she could see them. The upholstery was deep and velvety. She hoped the rainwater she was dripping wouldn't ruin it. Outside, the car was almost ordinary looking, some dark shade of gray.

"Your car seems very sedate for a sports hero's car," she said.

"Looks more like a minister's car than yours, doesn't it? Keeps the police from bothering me, except when they get close enough to see my face."

"Then they recognize you for a famous sports star."

"No, then they notice I'm black, and they pull me over." *Ah*, she thought, *race paranoia.* The engine started right up, whisper-quiet, not like her old Nova.

"They don't recognize you?" she said.

"Only around Philadelphia, and then all they want to do is give me a hard time about quitting baseball, like your boyfriend Dave."

"Dave isn't my boyfriend."

"So I try not to speed too much, at least not where they can catch me."

As they drove over the one-lane bridge to the main road, her nonboyfriend Dave Dogg appeared in his own car, headed back toward the field. She rolled down the window and called to him: "Was Freddy home when you got there?"

He shook his head no and drove on. Just as well. If they'd stopped to talk, he would have given her a lecture about losing Freddy, or maybe about the evils of civilians meddling in police business. *I do the best I can.* Even in her head she was arguing with him, and he hadn't said a word. *Lost Freddy.*

Mac Barrow pulled out onto the highway and headed toward town, driving just a little bit too fast for Mother Grey's taste. In the twinkling of an eye they were back in town, waiting for the light to change at Bridge and Main streets.

The yellow convertible was waiting on the other side of the intersection, with its top still up against the last drops of rain. A throbbing sound was coming from it, so strong as to seem to be the car's means of propulsion. You wouldn't think of it as music. The driver beat on the steering wheel with the heel of one hand in time to the boom, boom.

"That child must be stone deaf," Mother Grey said.

Mac Barrow said, "People inside the car with the bass turned up that far can't hear it. The sound is all on the outside."

"Wasteful," Mother Grey remarked. But wait, wasn't that the missing Dawn Hudson in the passenger seat?

The light changed. The yellow car moved on. "There goes Dawn Hudson," Mother Grey said. Where were Kreevitch and his minions when you needed them? Harassing old men, was where.

"It's okay," Mac said. "She came home today. Rochelle came and told Tommy right before the game started."

"I should have told Rochelle about that boy in the car," Mother Grey said.

"You can't be responsible for everyone in town."

Responsible for everyone in town? How irritating; the man was beginning to sound like Dave. "This is not New York City, you know," she said to him. "We look out for each other here. That's what makes small-town life work."

"Okay," he said.

"And I don't feel responsible for everyone in town."

"Okay."

So Tommy Hudson took Freddy home. Maybe he took him to his own home for some reason. "Can you drop me at the Hudsons', Mac? I'd feel better if I knew that Freddy was safe."

"Okay," he said. "Small-town life, right? Not like you feel responsible." He made a smooth U-turn, cut down a side street, and pulled up a half-block from the three-story brick row house where the Hudsons lived.

Which was as close as he could get. Clustered in front, blocking the street, were three police cars and an ambulance, all with their lights flashing, and the Channel 6 news van.

"We can probably take these sandbags down now," Schwartz said. "The immediate threat is past." Danny gazed out over the backyard of the halfway house, thinking, *Good.* It would be pleasant to have a normal backyard again. Schwartz had murdered a number of bushes to install his entrenchments.

"I'm glad the threat is over," he said. "But what makes you think the threat is over?"

"The ranger has been eliminated."

"Oh," Danny said. "Right. Let's get to it, then." If they were lucky, Mother Grey would not come back here and notice the mess before they had it more or less cleaned up. There might be penalties for committing hydrangeacide at a state-sponsored facility.

They had removed the first layer of sandbags and were working on the second when out of the sky came a throbbing sound. Schwartz looked up.

"Black helicopters," he said. Actually there was only one. "Take cover, I'll get the pistol."

By the time Schwartz reappeared waving his gat, Danny had gotten a good look at the helicopter. It wasn't black at all, but white, and it bore a big red cross.

"It's medical, Schwartz," Danny said. "It won't hurt you. Give me that." He took the gun out of Schwartz's hand, not by prying it from his dead fingers, the way it said in the bumper sticker that Schwartz had stuck on his headboard, not having a car, but by gently removing it from fingers whose mind was someplace else.

"Where's it going?" Schwartz was still twitching with suspicion.

"Schoolyard, probably," Danny said. "That's where they usually pick up the wounded."

"Damn," said Schwartz, becoming more excited. "The wounded. Let's go see."

They ran out front and down the street in time to see it all, the white helicopter coming down, the ambulance driving onto the field, the crowd gathering, the Channel 6 camera crew pressing in, the squad loading a blanket-covered victim onto the 'copter.

Old Horace Burkhardt was standing on the edge of the crowd with his hands in his pockets. "Who's hurt?" Danny asked him.

"Coach Hudson's wife."

"What happened to her?"

"Robbery. Somebody shot her and cleaned out her purse."

"Will she make it?"

"They think so. She was hit once in the arm and once in the chest, but I've seen men recover from worse chest wounds than that."

"In the war, right?" said Schwartz.

"You bet," said Horace. "The real war. So they'll take her to Camden, get her fixed up. Shame." Danny couldn't figure out whether the old man was saying it was a shame she was shot or a shame she was likely to recover.

With a great roaring and swooshing the helicopter rose straight up and then swooped off southward. Twigs, leaves, and dirt spun in the air. When the dust had settled, Schwartz grabbed Danny by the arm.

"Come on," he said. "They're interviewing people for the news. Let's go and watch."

"Maybe they'll let us talk," Danny said, though he really couldn't think what he would say. When they got close enough to hear, the news lady was asking Mrs. Hudson's husband and son how they felt now that their mom had been shot, while two policemen tried to shoo her away.

Abruptly, Mother Vinnie stepped between

Rochelle Hudson's family and the news team. She told them who she was.

"I have something important to say," she said.

They must have decided to let her talk. Into the microphone, into the camera, the news lady said, "I'm speaking with the Reverend Lavinia Grey, the vicar of St. Bede's, Fishersville. Reverend Grey, what do you think of the rash of shootings that have taken place here in the quiet town of Fishersville this week?"

"I think this sort of violence has gone on long enough," Mother Vinnie said, "both here in Fishersville and in every other part of the country. How many have to be killed before people begin to behave sensibly about guns?"

"But what can be done?" said the news lady. She was playing up to Mother Vinnie's sermonizing.

"We need better handgun laws. But before that happens, the gun owners must take more care. First of all, if you must keep guns, keep them unloaded and locked up where no children or burglars can get at them. Secondly, if you don't need a gun—and who needs a gun?—get rid of it."

Danny looked down at the pistol in his hand, suddenly embarrassed, as though his fly were open. Fortunately no one had noticed him holding it so far. He tucked it under his arm, hoping to hide it.

Mother Vinnie went on airing her views about violence and handguns to the Channel 6 camera. She gave a very persuasive speech, full of passion and compelling rhetoric. At last she said, "You citizens can put an end to this insanity. Bring your guns to

St. Bede's. I'll take them, no questions asked, and the killing will stop."

"Thank you, Mother Lavinia Grey of St. Bede's, Fishersville."

The red light went off. "Will that be on television?" Mother Grey asked.

"Think so," the newswoman said. "We may have to cut it some. Depends on what other news they have tonight, how much time they can let me have for it." She and the cameraman disappeared into the truck.

Danny, meanwhile, was standing entranced. Mother Vinnie's speech had thrilled him to the very core, and now the gun he was trying to hide under his arm seemed obscene. He would take it to the church. Schwartz was the last person who should have it.

Horace Burkhardt appeared by his side and began to cackle at him. "You know, son, seeing you trying to hide that pistol reminds me of an old story."

"What pistol?" said Danny. He could feel himself blushing.

"It's about the woman who lost the top of her bathing suit."

"What makes you think I have a pistol? I wouldn't carry a pistol." He pulled the fabric of his shirt around it. Now, surely, it couldn't be seen. But wait! Now the muzzle was pointing into the crowd. What if it went off, injuring some innocent person? He readjusted his position, hunching a little to the left.

"She loses the top of her bathing suit, see, and so

she figures she'll just go and get in the water before anybody notices, and she folds her arms across her chest like this and starts running toward the lake." The old man crossed his arms on his chest.

"I have to go," said Danny, edging away from him, readjusting the position of the gun again.

"And this little boy comes along and says—hee! hee!"

" 'Scuse me." He had to get rid of this thing. He turned his face toward St. Bede's and set out walking at a good clip.

The old man followed.

"He says, 'Lady, I know you're going to drown those puppies, but can I have the one with the pink nose?' "

There was no getting rid of him. "So what's your point?"

"My point is, son, where are you going with that gun?"

"I'm taking it to St. Bede's, the way Mother Vinnie said to, if you must know," Danny said, and he plodded doggedly on.

"Why don't you let me take it?" said Horace. "I'm going that way anyhow. I live almost next door."

Danny stopped walking and looked at the old man. Why not give it to him, after all? Old people could usually be trusted.

"Okay," Danny said. He untangled the pistol from his shirt and handed it over carefully, keeping the barrel pointed at the ground. It was as though an enormous weight had been lifted from him.

15

By the time Mother Grey finished talking to the TV news people, the crowd had begun to thin out. She was still looking for Freddy. Way over by the side of the school stood a boy in an Angels uniform, all by himself, but it turned out to be poor Garrett Hudson.

"Have you seen Freddy?" she asked him.

"Can't say I have."

"Where's your dad? I need to talk to him."

"Over there. He's . . . um—in custody."

"Oh."

"They put him in a cop car. They won't let us go home anyhow until they're finished using our house for a crime scene."

"Garrett, you're going to need somewhere to stay until this is all cleared up. Why don't you come with me? I have an extra bed at the rectory."

"No, thanks. I'm supposed to go to Aunt Marla's."

"Come along with us anyway," said Mac. "We'll get a pizza."

"No, I'm okay."

"Poor kid," said Mac, as they slogged across the wet schoolyard.

"What a terrible thing to happen," said Mother Grey.

"How about you?" he said. "Would you like to share a pizza?"

It was a terrible thing. The worst of it was that it was all so mindless and random, seemingly. Who would be next? And where was Freddy? . . . Pizza? "Let's see whether they'll let me talk to Tommy. I want to find out whether he knows where Freddy could have gotten to."

"Okay."

"And I need to change my clothes." Mother Grey was still soaking wet from the rainstorm. "I must look a fright," she said, "to be going on television."

"You looked wonderful," said Mac. "You were— how shall I put this?—very lovely, and very theatrical. An avenging angel of peace. Your speech will be great on TV."

"Do you think they'll run it?"

"I'll be surprised if they don't. And it was really persuasive. If I had a handgun, I'd give it to you in a minute. What will you do with all the firearms?"

Would people bring her their firearms? She hadn't thought that far ahead. "I don't know. Give them to the police. Bury them in the undercroft."

"Start an army," he suggested. "Onward, Christian soldiers."

"We don't sing that anymore."

Madge Whitfield, the reporter from the *Clarion*, stopped them on the sidewalk and asked Mother Grey's opinion of the recent shootings. Her notepad was in her hand, her face expectant; she wanted color for a sidebar.

"Guns are doing these shootings," said Mother Grey. "For my part, I would like to see all firearms out of private hands, but handguns particularly."

"What about hunters?" said the reporter. "What about the overpopulation of deer?"

"Anyone who would use a handgun to shoot a deer needs counseling," said Mother Grey. "My office hours are from two to five on Mondays, Thursdays, and Fridays. I can be reached at St. Bede's; the number is in the book." *Hope that's colorful enough.* The reporter thanked her and moved on.

"Do you want to meet me at the pizza parlor?" she said to Mac. "Or do you want to stay while I try to talk to Tommy?"

"I want to be around to see what you do next."

She looked for Jack Kreevitch, but he was off someplace dealing with the drunk-and-disorderly Rex Perskie. Tommy sat handcuffed in the back of a Fishersville police car, under the protection of Patrolman Jim Finn, who stood outside, leaning on the car. They let Tommy keep the window rolled down; even after the violent storm of the hour before, the heat was oppressive.

"Is it all right if we talk to Tommy?" Mother Grey said.

Patrolman Finn glanced around, probably to

check on whether anyone who could give him a hard time might be watching—Cranmer, for instance. Seeing nobody, he said, "Yeah, sure. Don't give him nothin', or touch him or like that."

"How ya doin', Tommy," said Mac.

"Not real great." There were bloodstains on his shirt. "Mother Vinnie, I want to thank you for getting that TV crew out of our faces."

"The least I could do," she said. "How is Rochelle? Is she—?"

"Like I told the law enforcement officers, Rochelle was out cold when I found her, losing blood. She was hit in the arm and in the chest. She couldn't say who did it, she couldn't say nothin'."

"So they arrested you," Mac said.

"I don't know what they think I did with the gun, or the credit cards and money that whoever it was took out of her purse."

"Do you need anything?" said Mac. "Do you have a lawyer? Is there anybody you want us to call?"

"I don't think there's anything. Rochelle's mother is flying in from St. Augustine. She said she'd get me a lawyer and make bail. Garrett is going to stay with Jack and Marla and the kids while I'm at the hospital with Rochelle. I just wish I knew where Dawn was."

"You guys, here comes Cranmer," said Jim Finn. "Make it short."

"Do you know what happened to Freddy Kane?" Mother Grey said. "Rex Perskie said he left the ball field with you."

"Freddy." His face changed, as though he suddenly remembered some difficulty. "Oh, yeah, he did."

"And?"

"I brought him home with me in the storm, and then . . . Jesus, I don't know, he must have left and gone home."

"Why did you bring him to your house?"

He shook his head, a man trying to waken from a bad dream. "Poor little kid, I forgot all about him when I found Rochelle."

"Something was going on between you and Freddy, wasn't there, Tommy?" Mother Grey said.

"Between me and Freddy," he said. "Sure."

"What was it?" said Mac.

"I needed to talk to him. I've been trying to get up the nerve to have a talk with him for days. I've even been following him around."

He looked from one to the other of them, his face earnest and troubled, and Mother Grey noticed for the first time something about the way his eyebrows grew. And the shape of his nose, and the dent in the middle of his chin. Even with his hairline receding, the family resemblance was there for the careful observer. It seemed surprising to her now that she had never seen it before.

"Freddy is your son," she guessed.

He nodded. "I've never been able to do anything for him particularly; Saraleigh wouldn't let me near him except for the ball team. But then here came this jerk Rex Perskie threatening him. Can you beat that? A little kid."

Cranmer was coming up the street, looking grim. Jim Finn muttered, "Cheese it, cheese it."

"Big man, threatens a little kid," Tommy went on, not hearing him. "And so I thought, 'I can't give him any money, I can't give him my name, but I can do this for him.'"

"So you thrashed Rex." Mac gave Mother Grey an odd look, and she thought, *Thrashed—how Victorian I must sound.*

"Yeah, I beat the—I thrashed him a good one. Trust me, he had it coming. And you should have seen the kid's face. It was like Christmas, like I was Santa Claus." A deep breath, slowly exhaled. "Then I told him I was his father. The kid needs someone in his corner. Saraleigh's husband is never around."

"So then you took him home with you."

"We needed to talk about it."

"Before you . . . beat Rex up—did he try to blackmail you about Bunker Todd's leg?"

A short, mirthless laugh. "Some blackmail. Everybody in town knows I broke Bunker Todd's leg."

"What's this, a tea party?" said Cranmer. "What's going on here, Finn?"

"I just wish I knew whether Dawn was okay," said Tommy, pulling his head in the window.

"Dawn is safe," Mother Grey said. "We saw her a little while ago driving around with Randy Todd."

"Thank God. If you happen to see her again, tell her to go stay at Marla and Jack's tonight," Tommy said.

"We'll tell her," Mac said.

"Let's get this prisoner to the county jail," said

Cranmer. "Let's not be hanging around Fishersville socializing."

Mother Grey and Mac went to the pizzeria to socialize. First they stopped at the rectory for some dry clothes for Mother Grey. She actually considered for a moment putting on a clerical collar with her jeans and shirt, but she thought, *Whatever for?* She was only going out for pizza, it was a social occasion and not professional, after all. Had she but known how many times she would wish she had worn the collar before she got back to the rectory, or how many hours it would be, she would have at least walked Towser.

There were four pizzerias in the town of Fishersville, one for every thousand of the population, the same as the number of volunteer fire companies. The one in the center of town was the teen hangout. There were two on the north end: the family place, where they also had things like antipasto and cheesecake but they didn't start the pizza ovens before four o'clock, and the fast place. The fourth one was across the highway. Mother Grey had never eaten there. They went to the fast place because they had to get busy and find Freddy.

"Do you like anchovies?" Mac asked.

"Sure do."

"Extra cheese?"

"Yep."

"Garlic?"

"By all means." So he ordered a large pie with

anchovies, garlic, and extra cheese, and while they waited for it to cook, they drank Orangina out of little bulbous bottles. They were the only customers in the place.

Somehow, sometime, Mother Grey had stopped expecting Mac Barrow to turn into a serial drive-by shooter or whatever it was she had feared when first he introduced himself and asked her for a key to St. Bede's. If anything, he was turning out to be more correct and proper in his views and behavior than her usual associates, black, white, or indifferent. Still, a man who will eat anchovies and garlic on his pizza can't be too much of a stiff, and she found herself able to relax in his company.

He wanted to talk about the shootings.

"So who do you like for the killer?" he said. "I don't believe Tommy did those shootings. Do you?"

"No. Of course, you know him better than I do."

"They say he has a terrible temper," said Mac. "I've never seen him lose it. Jack Kreevitch tells a story that was supposed to have happened at his cousin's wedding, where one of the groom's fraternity brothers ran into Tommy's new car in the rescue squad parking lot. Said it took five guys to get them apart. Tommy had to spend the night in jail."

"That would have been in his youth, surely."

"It was two years ago. Vinnie, he is in his youth. How old do you think he is?"

"Never thought about it."

"He's thirty-one. Jack says he and Rochelle were married right out of high school."

The pizza came, smelly, cheesy, and succulent.

Mac went back to the cooler and returned with another round of Oranginas.

"Of course Tommy did quite a job on Rex Perskie," Mother Grey said. "Did you see his eye? But that isn't the same thing as sneaking around plinking at people from behind bushes."

"I agree. It's not his style," Mac said. They addressed the food in silence for a while.

"What does Jack think?" Mother Grey said. "Have you talked to him about it?"

"He told me some details, but he didn't mention any suspects."

"Tell me."

"First of all, both Bunker Todd and the ranger were killed by twenty-two-caliber bullets from the same gun."

"Okay. Probably we can assume that the same gun wounded Rochelle."

"Then he said there was a burglary in town, right before this all started happening, where a bunch of twenty-two-caliber pistols were stolen."

"Dave told me about that. One of them was used in a robbery in Trenton. The clerk was killed. He said they found a hat at the burgled house that they thought was Freddy's."

"So that same burglary was probably where our murder weapon came from, would be my guess."

"My word. You don't think Freddy—?"

"No, no," he said. "Freddy's a good kid. But somebody—"

"Who benefits?" she said. "That's what you're supposed to ask. Always presuming that there was some sort of logic behind these attacks, is there anyone who benefits from these deaths?"

"What about Horace?" said Mac. "He seemed delighted to get out of his contract with Bunker Todd."

"Yes, but he seemed surprised, to put it mildly. You don't think that was all an act, do you?"

"I wouldn't have said so. You know, though, Jack said Horace was overheard fighting with the ranger the other day about that dog."

"Everybody fought with the ranger about their dogs."

"True, and everybody hated Bunker Todd."

"What about the Little League coaches, then?" she said. "Jack, for that matter? Or what about you?"

"I didn't have anything against the ranger," he said. "I don't even like dogs. Are you going to eat that last piece?"

"No, thanks. I'm full. To tell you the truth, I like Rex for it, he's the ugliest man in town, disposition-wise. Unfortunately, he has an ironclad alibi. We saw him ourselves, falling-down drunk in a closet at the other end of town."

"Do you want to give Saraleigh a call, see whether Freddy turned up yet?"

"Yes," she said. She had a quarter. Saraleigh answered the phone right away, but no, she hadn't seen Freddy.

"Mac and I will look around town some more for him. If we don't turn him up in the next half hour, maybe we should report him missing to the police."

"I might do that anyway," Saraleigh said. "Call me if you hear anything."

"I will." She hung up the telephone.

"No news?" Mac said.

"None," she said.

"Let's go see if we can find Dawn," said Mac. "We can tell her what happened to her mother, and give her Tommy's message about spending the night at Jack and Marla's. She might even be able to tell us where to find Freddy."

16

The yellow convertible was parked in the yard beside Bunker Todd's house by the bike trail, still making high-volume bass noises. Mac pulled up and parked beside it. Nobody was in the driver's seat.

The backseat was full of Rottweilers, and they all began to bark as Mac and Mother Grey got out of the car. Mother Grey saw the girl in the passenger seat, her hand and arm hanging out the window, beating time on the side of the car. She called out to her but could not make herself heard above the radio and the dogs.

"Dawn!" she called again. "I need to talk to you!" The dogs barked all the louder.

"Help. Help me."

That was no dog.

Banging, banging on the trunk lid. "Let me out."

"Freddy?" Mac called.

"Coach Mac! Help!"

"Jesus, he's locked in the trunk," said Mac. Dawn Hudson looked up and saw them then. Her face was scarcely human.

"Brutus! Kill!" she shouted, opening the right rear door. Three Rottweilers tumbled out and went straight for Mac's throat. Racism? Sexism? In any case, they didn't try to bite Mother Grey, who nonetheless shrieked at them and grabbed for their collars.

In the door of the house Randy Todd appeared, carrying two sodas and a big bag of fried chicken. "Brutus! Siegfried! Shatzie! Sit!" The dogs backed down. Dawn Hudson slid over to the driver's seat and turned the key.

"Are you all right?" Randy Todd asked Mac.

"Tore my jacket," Mac said, inspecting himself. "No broken skin."

"Dunno why they did that, my dogs don't usually—Hey! What the—? Dawn! What are you doing!" What she was doing was putting the car in gear and scratching out of the driveway.

"Come on," Mac said, dragging Mother Grey back to the Beemer. "It's high-speed car-chase time." He started the engine, and they were off in a burst of neck-snapping acceleration.

The girl was doing movie things, strange power slides that caused the fat rear end of the old Pontiac to fishtail all over the gravel road. Mac did other movie things trying to keep up with her. Frantically fastening her seat belt, Mother Grey felt as though she had stumbled into a James Bond film.

Burning rubber, or maybe burning oil, the yel-

low convertible roared onto the main road and raced
out of town. Mac chased her at top speed. It wasn't
like a TV car chase. First of all, this wasn't a six-lane
California freeway, only the road out of Fishersville—narrow, lined with rocky cliffs, and by and
large deserted. The gravel trucks that carried the
mountain away were the only steady traffic on this
road. Just now they weren't running. Nobody here
but Dawn and Mac.

Still, they were making an uncommon racket;
the police would be after them soon. With a squeal of
tires Dawn blasted up the ramp onto the interstate.

"Maybe you should just follow at a discreet distance," Mother Grey suggested as she clung to the
door and the dashboard. Mac was definitely exceed-
ing the speed limit. "If you get her excited, she might
crash the car and hurt Freddy."

"Hush."

She hushed. They were gaining on the girl, getting close enough to hear the throb of the car stereo.
Driving this fast was quite exciting, Mother Grey re-
flected, once you got used to it. Still, she was afraid
to sit back and let go of the dashboard. Mac passed a
car, then a truck. There was traffic now, plodding
along almost at a standstill, it seemed.

"Uh, oh," Mac said, slowing down abruptly.

"What?" she said. "What?!" Out of gas? Mechani-
cal malfunction? Then she heard the siren and saw
the reflection of flashing lights. Mac pulled the car
over to the side of the road.

A huge trooper appeared in the driver-side window. All Mother Grey could see of him was his belt

buckle and his white-as-in-Caucasian hands. "Could you step out of the car, please, sir?"

A sense of horrific déjà vu settled over her. She had experienced this scene before, on *True Stories of Real Cops*. Always before she had sided with the cops.

With a weary sigh, Mac stepped out of the Beemer.

"Let me see your hands, please, sir."

"Officer, did you see a yellow convertible, canary yellow, go by here? It's a kidnapping incident," he said to the cop.

"Put your hands on the top of the car, please." So he did, and the officer patted him down.

"Now the passenger. Can I ask you to get out of the car, miss?"

She knew how this went; she had seen it a hundred times; next the officer would make her grovel in the dirt, and then he would kneel on her neck.

"I'm the Reverend Lavinia Grey from St. Bede's, Fishersville," she explained to him, in her most dignified tones. "We're trying to catch a young girl who has stolen a car and kidnapped her little brother." Oh, why hadn't she dressed in clericals before she left town?

"Just put your hands on top of the vehicle," said the officer. He had a nametag on his chest—Schoenwald, it said.

He fished Mac's wallet out of his pocket and read the driver's license. "Mac Barrow," he said. "I'll be damned."

"It's really very urgent, officer," Mother Grey

said. "The driver is only fourteen; she's locked her little brother in the trunk of the car. It's so hot today, I'm afraid he's—"

"I'm going to have to ticket you for speeding, sir. Do you have any idea how fast you were going?"

"No, actually I haven't," Mac said. Meanwhile, many miles down the highway, the yellow convertible sped away and away, clear out of the realm of human consciousness.

"Mac Barrow," said Schoenwald. "How about that. So tell me. Why the hell did you quit baseball?"

"Personal reasons," Mac said.

"Just stay there for a minute. Don't move, either of you. Keep your hands on top of the car." He went back to the police car and used the radio, calling for backup or running them through the computer for warrants or whatever it was they did. More minutes passed.

"This is too humiliating," Mother Grey whispered.

"Tell me about it," Mac said.

As Dave Dogg drove up to the Todd residence, he saw that the driveway was empty of cars, if full of Rottweilers, and Randy Todd was standing in the middle of it gnawing on a piece of chicken. Dave leaned out of the driver-side window and asked the youth, "What's going on?"

"Damned if I know. This mixed couple in a gray BMW pulls into the driveway, and my girlfriend sics the dogs on them and takes off, leaving me here with the food."

"Mixed couple," said Dave. "I assume by that you mean a sports hero and a priest."

"Whatever, a black man and a white woman, maybe they were a news team. Hope she doesn't wreck my Pontiac. It took me three years to get it fixed up like that."

"Good job too," said Dave.

"Thanks." He ate another chicken leg, throwing the bone to the dogs. Two of them growled and tussled over it. "I only left the keys in the car so she could listen to the music."

"Do you know why she ran?"

"No. Do you?"

"I think so. Your girlfriend is a fugitive."

"From what?"

"Justice. This afternoon her mother was found shot."

A flicker of intelligence crossed his features. "Holy Christ. So that's why she wouldn't let me in the house."

"So what did she do, call you for a ride out of town?"

"We were supposed to go to the shore this weekend after my dad's funeral. She said she was going to ask her mother if it was okay."

"Guess the answer was no."

"Holy Christ."

"Are you aware that Dawn Hudson is only fourteen?"

"Fourteen?"

"How old did you think she was?"

"She told me she was eighteen."

"Not only does she not have a license, she isn't old enough to drive," Dave pointed out.

"I didn't mean for her to drive. She said she wanted to listen to the radio."

"Do you happen to know where she might be headed?"

"No."

"Also," Dave said, "I wonder if you'd mind coming with me to City Hall. There are some police officers there who might want to ask you a few questions."

"Are you saying I'm under arrest?"

"Not that I know of. But you might be of help. Wanna come along?"

"Sure, why not." He put the dogs in the house and folded himself into the front seat of Dave's car. "Want some chicken?"

"Thanks," said Dave. It was pretty good chicken, if greasy.

"Here, you might as well take her soda too," Randy said.

The county homicide police were still swarming all over Tommy and Rochelle Hudson's neat brick house. Jack Kreevitch sat on the stoop, staring into space and holding a portable telephone to his ear, while into his other ear Detective Cranmer poured his ill temper.

"So she didn't say who shot her," Cranmer said

for the hundredth time, not even pretending anymore that he believed it.

"I told you, Tommy found her unconscious," Kreevitch said.

"Yes, he said that, didn't he? He also had some strange tale about a gun that somebody found in the sewer, how he brought it home and now it isn't there anymore. Somehow he never mentioned it to the police, finding this gun in the sewer a hundred feet away from a shooting death, when the murder weapon hadn't been recovered."

"He was preoccupied, his daughter ran away." It seemed perfectly logical to Kreevitch. Who collects evidence, when he doesn't even know there's a crime going on? It's not like Tommy was a cop—he was just an ordinary guy, a former line foreman at the defunct baby food factory. "Charlie, can I talk to you later about this? I'm waiting for these people to—Hello? Hello?" He was almost sure he heard the voice of a human being, but no, it must have been another recording.

"I know you like Tommy, and he's your brother-in-law and all, but he had motive and opportunity. And he's known to be a violent person," Cranmer said.

"What do you mean?" said Kreevitch. *What have you found out? Who has been talking?*

"His wife was running around with that guy Bunker Todd. A concerned citizen just explained the whole thing to me. Do you know Hudson took a baseball bat and broke the guy's leg? Happened last month."

"Concerned citizen?" *All our operators are assist
ing other customers. Please wait, and your call will be
answered in its turn.*

"This guy you arrested for vagrancy or whatever
it was. He's down at City Hall running his mouth. So,
Jack, what do they think of your sister's chances? Is
she gonna pull through?"

"Dunno. I'll call the hospital right after I talk to
these— Hello?" This time he was sure the voice was
that of a live human. "No, please don't put me back
on hold. Hello?"

A plainclothes policewoman came out of the
house carrying a plastic evidence bag and bran-
dished it in Cranmer's face.

"Look at these," she said.

Cranmer took the bag and examined it closely,
then handed it back. "Twenty-two shells. How about
that," he said. "The small-bore killer strikes again."

Oh, that's real funny. "Could you be quiet a minute, Charlie? I'm trying to report Rochelle's credit
cards stolen, so the next time one of the cards is used
we can trace whoever attacked her," he said. "They
keep putting me on hold."

"You're wasting your time. Tommy's our man,"
Cranmer said. "Where we have him, he's not gonna
do a whole lot of charging."

"Hello! Yes, you can help me. My sister's credit
cards have been stolen. No, I don't know the numbers. Her name is Rochelle Hudson."

17

"**M**ore eye makeup," Dawn said. "I like that turquoise color you're using, but you haven't put enough on. I can hardly see it."

The blue-smocked cosmetologist stood back and checked the results of her work. "Sometimes a subtle effect is better on a young person," she said. "Especially on a face with a great deal of natural beauty, like yours."

"I want it good and dark," said Dawn. Why would a person want a makeover, if she was happy with her natural look?

"Dark," said the cosmetologist. "Very well." Gently she brushed more shadow onto Dawn's eyelids. It almost tickled. Dawn opened her eyes and looked in the mirror.

Foxy. The reek from her arms was marvelous; each part of her skin smelled of a different perfume sample. The kid in the trunk could wait. This was too much fun to pass up.

"Yes, it's good, I like that," Dawn said. "I'll take some of that and also the mascara and the lipstick. Do you have any matching nail polish?"

"As a matter of fact we have a special this week. If you buy seventy dollars' worth of Madame Defarge skin care products, we're offering a complimentary faux crocodile travel bag with nail polish, cuticle defender, eyelash treatment, and two ounces of Fleurs de Bastille cologne. It's a fifty-dollar value."

A travel bag. Good. "Let me have a three-ounce jar of the age-defying creme, then, and some sunscreen; that should bring it up almost to seventy-five."

"Will that be cash or charge?"

"Charge," said Dawn, and gave her the Visa card she had taken from her mother's purse.

Then she went up the escalator and bought some interesting lingerie, a couple of cool outfits, and six bathing suits in different colors. Almost all of them fit into the faux crocodile travel bag.

When she got her packages out to the parking lot, Freddy Kane was banging on the trunk lid of Randy's car. "Shut up in there," she said. "I told you."

"It's hot in here! I'm thirsty! I have to go to the bathroom!"

"I'm not gonna baby-sit you. I hate baby-sitting."

"Let me out!"

"Shut up!"

"Please! I'm going to die!"

"All right, we'll go to McDonald's. But don't try anything."

* * *

In McDonald's, Freddy went into the men's room and tried something. He tried asking one of the locals for help.

"She's not my sister. Or well, yeah, she's my sister, but she's keeping me prisoner because I caught her shooting her mother."

"Yeah, right."

"Or anyway I saw her with a smoking gun. I'm not kidding. She killed three people last week."

"Get lost, kid."

So Dawn made him get back in the car again, but she let him ride in the front seat this time so he could hold her hamburgers and stuff while she drove. After a while he found that tooling along in a convertible was exciting. The wind blew his hair back over his eyes, not back off his forehead like you'd think, but the phone poles were just whizzing by, and he figured they must be going really fast.

A round thing showed over the horizon of scrubby pines that he realized was the Ferris wheel at Great Adventure. If she stopped at McDonald's, maybe she would be willing to stop here too.

Worth a try. "Hey, Dawn! It's Great Adventure! Can we stop at Great Adventure?"

"For what?"

"The rides! Look, it's the Ferris wheel."

"They'll have lots of rides when we get to Wildwood." She ate up her hamburger and threw the wrapper into the road.

"Can I go on a ride in Wildwood?" he said.

"Okay. One ride."

"Thanks. You're a good sister."

"I'm not your sister."

"Yes, you are."

"How do you figure?"

"Tommy is my dad. He told me so."

"Yeah, right." It was not his day to be believed.

"Why did you shoot your mother?" he asked when he had finished his soda.

"She was a drunken slut."

"She was?"

"It wasn't my fault. She forced me to do it."

"What did she do, say, 'Here, Dawn, take this gun and shoot me, or else you're grounded for a week'?"

"She might as well have. I need a life, you know. I'm a human being."

"Oh. Okay."

"She wouldn't let me see Randy, if you must know."

"Isn't Randy going to be annoyed that you stole his car?"

"I borrowed it. If he really loves me, he'll understand."

"Sure, Dawn. Sure."

On they drove, on interstates, on smaller roads, through the middle of various small towns, and way out into the country, until it seemed as though it must be suppertime. Dawn stopped at a little store, one of those places that needed paint with two old gas pumps out in front. She got gas, more food, and a map of South Jersey.

The woman behind the counter was fat and

dumb-looking, but Freddy tried anyway. He took a ball-point pen out of a cup of pens for sale and wrote on a blotter in front of the cash register: *Help! I am being held prisoner! The girl with me is Dawn Hudson, she just killed three people and she's taking me against my will to Wildwood, New Jersey!* and he signed it *Freddy Kane.* The woman stared at him; there were puffs of flesh under her eyes. Maybe she wasn't too impressed with the way he looked either. His uniform was sweaty and stained, his stirrups fallen down around his ankles.

"You gonna buy that pen?" she said.

"Don't have any money," he said.

"Then keep your little hands off the pens," the woman said. "They have a wax seal on them to keep them fresh. You write with them, you break the seal, and they dry out."

"Sorry," he said.

"Go ahead and use the bathroom," Dawn said. "I'll be waiting right here. I'd like to charge these things, please," she said to the dumb woman. As it turned out, there was no window in the bathroom, so he couldn't escape that way.

"Let's go," said Dawn. She gave him a couple of Slim Jims and spread the map out in the front seat of the car. "Now, I wonder how you get to Wildwood from here," she said.

"Garden State Parkway," Freddy offered.

"No good. They have tollbooths. Someone might be looking for this car."

* * *

By the time they drove across the bridge over the bay and down the main drag into the craziness that was Wildwood, the sun had gone down in a bruise-purple sky. Wildwood seemed to be a whole city of teenagers, teenage heaven. Clumps of them stood talking under the streetlights. You could see the lights of the boardwalk from the motel that Dawn drove into. Grown-ups ran the motel, but maybe the grown-ups were only there to sell the kids food and souvenirs and to keep the rides running.

"I'd like a room for me and my little brother," she said to the man in the office.

"Actually I'm her half-brother," Freddy said to the man. "She's kidnapping me. There's a gun in her bag, she's killed three people—"

"Back in the trunk, Freddy? Trunkie-wunkie?"

"What's that, son?" the man said.

"Nothing."

"Forty-three," the man said. "Here's the key."

The room smelled of mildew, and the air conditioner was very loud. Again there was no back way out of the bathroom.

"I'm hungry," said Freddy.

"Have another Slim Jim."

"Let's go out. I want to see the boardwalk. You promised I could go on a ride."

"All right. But just to eat and one ride. And nothing funny, unless you want to spend the whole night in the trunk."

The boardwalk was endless—noise, lights, crowds of teenagers jostling and swooping at them on Rollerblades, pier after pier of rides. They found a booth with stools where a big bald-headed cook sliced meat for sandwiches, one of the grown-ups who catered to the kids. Freddy eyed the knife, but it was out of his reach.

"What do you want?" Dawn said.

"Pizza."

"They don't have pizza."

"How about a hamburger?"

"No hamburger."

"A sandwich?"

"Two cheese steaks, please," she said, "and a couple of Cokes."

There was a nickel on the counter at Freddy's place. Some fool had gone away without his change. Freddy picked it up, only to discover that the coin was completely covered with grease. It came off on his hands, on his clothes, everything. "Can I have a napkin?"

"In a minute," Dawn said. Freddy had never been so disgusted by money.

The stool by Freddy was empty, but pretty soon a big boy sat down there and started talking to them. He said he came from Philly and his name was Guido.

"I'm Mariel Defarge," Dawn said. "This is my little brother Harry."

Freddy decided to take another chance: "Actually her name is Dawn Hudson. I'm really only her half-brother. She killed three people this week, including her mother, and kidnapped me, and now she's on the run. Watch out for the gun in her bag."

"Your brother is a laugh riot," said Guido. "Where are you from?"

"Fishersville," said Freddy, at the same time Dawn was saying, "New York City."

Their cheese steaks came. Freddy ate his while Dawn and this guy leaned across him and deepened their acquaintance. The fog of teenager-breath made him uncomfortable.

" 'Scuse me, do you know where the bathroom is?" he said to Guido.

"Over there." The door was clearly visible from where they sat, but maybe there was a back way out.

"Come right back," said Dawn, with her hand in her bag. "I can always make it four."

"Right, er, Mariel," said Freddy.

Guido laughed. "You're not back in five minutes, she's goin' in after you, kid," he said.

It looked promising at first, but there was no back way out of this bathroom either, and the one guy who was in there was looking at him so funny that Freddy got right out of there without trying to ask him for help. His mother had warned him about weird guys in public bathrooms.

Back at the food booth, Guido gave him a roll of quarters and pointed out a nearby arcade. "Have a good time, little buddy," he said. "Me and your sister want to talk."

"I'm watching you," said Dawn. Probably she wasn't really. He looked over his shoulder at her when he got to the entrance to the arcade. It was impossible to tell.

Down the boardwalk about three hundred yards,

he almost thought he saw a policeman in the crowd. Was Dawn watching him? Or could he make a break for it, force his way through the pressing throng of teenagers, find the policeman, and tell him everything?

If it was a policeman. He glanced into the arcade.

The arcade had a Bloody Death game.

Bloody Death! And Freddy with a roll of quarters! Just a couple of games, or maybe till he got to level two. Then he would go find the police and tell his story all over again.

18

UNHOLY ANGELS

There was scarcely a moon that night, and as the crickets chirped in the darkness, the people of Fishersville crept to St. Bede's one by one and left their guns on the steps. Randy Todd brought in all his late father's firearms, even the AK-47, after drinking a six-pack and meditating on the evils of violence. Chick Reeker stole his brother Howie's pistol and put it in the pile after he found out that Howie had stolen his. Others in town, mostly mothers, cleaned out cabinets, drawers, and the top shelves of closets and brought what they found there to the church.

When Mother Grey came to open St. Bede's on Sunday morning, the birds were singing, the sun was peeping up over the horizon, and on the church steps lay a huge arsenal piled up almost as high as her knees. She had no idea there were so many firearms in Fishersville.

My word. What am I going to do with them?

Some were wrapped, and some were tagged to say where they had come from, but most were simply lying in a voiceless and vaguely threatening heap. Could all these be from Fishersville, or were people bringing them from out of town?

She went inside and called 911. "Send a truck over," she said. "All the guns in the world are on my doorstep."

The nearest police truck was at the county seat; all Fishersville had was cars and bicycles. "Unless we use an emergency rescue vehicle," the dispatcher said. "But they don't usually like to use those for other than life-threatening situations. This isn't an emergency, is it?"

Well, no, she supposed not. "How about the recycling truck?" said Mother Grey.

"On a Sunday? I don't think so," said the dispatcher. "Anyway you'll have to call Fishersville City Hall to arrange that, and they aren't open until tomorrow morning."

Now she was going to have to arrange some sort of convoy for these weapons to get them safely stored away in the hands of the proper authorities. Some of them might even be loaded. What if there was an accident? She went back outside and found Schwartz in his camouflage shorts rummaging in the contraband.

"An AK-47," he murmured. "Come to Papa, you sweet thing."

"Schwartz!" She succeeded in startling him. "Put it back now!"

"Aw, Mother Vinnie—"

"Instantly, Schwartz! Why, I'm ashamed of you. Whatever can you be thinking of?" She took the thing out of his hands.

"I'm thinking of Idaho, Mother Vinnie. This would come in so handy in the militia, when I go west."

"I'm sure you wouldn't be allowed to cross the state line with it. Now, stop daydreaming and help me carry these inside." A smile flitted across his face. "And if I catch you taking any of them you're going to be very, very sorry."

"Yes, ma'am."

Almost the only handgun in Fishersville still in private hands that morning was in the wrinkled and freckled old hands of Horace Burkhardt. *Surcease at last.* It was a beautiful morning; the same birds that serenaded St. Bede's twittered outside the window of his motor home. He stayed there almost all the time now, leaving his big empty house in the keeping of Sparky the dog.

He caressed the smooth blue surface of the pistol and thought, *Now what do I want to eat for my last meal?* Nothing fancy, it would have to be, since he didn't cook anymore and his daughter was still in Mexico, neglecting him. Maybe he would go out and eat, get some blueberry pancakes and sausage at Delio's.

But first the suicide note. He slipped Glenn Miller on the record player, and as the band struck up "A String of Pearls," he selected a clean piece of paper and a fresh felt-tip pen from the stationery drawer.

Dear Honey, he wrote. He had decided to address the note to Honey Kreevitch, the woman who had broken his heart, rather than *To Whom it May Concern*, because who did it concern, after all? Nobody. Nobody gave a hang about him.

On with the letter. Carefully he explained to Honey that it was all her fault. Hers and also his daughter's. And maybe the fault of the citizens of Fishersville, ungrateful wretches. It took several pages to say all that he had on his mind.

The babies were not allowed to run around in their usual fashion at mass that morning because of the pile of guns in the back of the church, which even under several tarpaulins and a sheet seemed to exert a strange pull on the children. Saraleigh kept both her girls firmly on her lap.

The church was almost half full, not even counting the sector occupied by the guns; all the usual congregants were in attendance, as well as a few strangers. It was Mac Barrow's first Sunday as organist, and Mother Grey was very pleased with him. The congregation sang lustily and with a semblance of good cheer. Still, everyone was worried and unhappy. During the Prayers of the People, they all prayed for the safety of Freddy.

After dismissal, Jack Kreevitch appeared at the door. He had gotten hold of a pickup truck from somewhere and was proposing to carry the guns away. "Unless you want to start a revolution or something," he said to Mother Grey. He pulled back the covering over the heap. "Looks like you could do a lot of damage with these."

"Take them away," said Mother Grey. "Do you have any news of Freddy?"

"Yes. That's the other reason I'm here, is to tell Saraleigh. We think Dawn took him to Wildwood."

"Wildwood!" Saraleigh said.

"He left a note in a minimart in the pines, where she charged some stuff on her mother's card. The local police found it. He said she was taking him to Wildwood."

"That's wonderful!" said Mother Grey. "I guess. Have they seen anything of him there? How big is Wildwood, anyway?"

Mac Barrow appeared in street clothes, having hung up his choirmaster's robe in the sacristy. "This time of year there's a million kids in Wildwood," he said. "Every kid in South Philly who can get a ride is there. Let me help you with these guns." He picked up two of them, not with comfort or familiarity, but more the way Mother Grey would hold a screaming baby. "Are we going to worry about fingerprints?" he asked.

"No, the hell with it," said Kreevitch. "Amnesty is amnesty. Later on we'll try to identify the stolen ones, just to see if we got 'em all. Dump 'em in the truck. But watch out. They may be loaded." The two men began to parade back and forth to the truck, carrying the guns in armfuls.

"So what are you doing about Freddy?"

Saraleigh demanded, following Kreevitch out to the truck.

"Wildwood is almost like an island. Dawn'll have to go over a bridge to get out again, if that's where they are. We'll find them. We've got the whole town staked out, looking for yellow convertibles. It's only a matter of time."

Freddy, half-carried back to the motel after an insane night of video gaming, fell into an exhausted sleep, broken after a long time by the sound of persistent hissing. He was dreaming of a huge snake, but when he woke up, there was none to be seen, only the accoutrements of a strange and empty motel room. The hissing continued, accompanied by giggles. Something smelled weird.

He got up and looked out the window. Dawn and her new friend Guido were out behind the cabin, dressed in bathing suits, spraying electric blue paint all over Randy Todd's car. Sometimes they squirted each other. Gross.

Dimly he remembered the arcade, the endless Bloody Death game, which he almost beat, the quarters going in, the other kids cheering, somebody giving him a beer. It tasted terrible, but he drank it. He was supposed to get a cop and save himself. But he forgot.

He picked up the phone. "Help," he said, when the motel man answered. "I'm a prisoner. Call the police "

"You again," said the motel man. "Listen, kid, I'm busy. I ain't got time for your stupid gags."

"Okay, what about some breakfast?" said Freddy.

"No room service here."

"Wildwood."

"Yeah, that's what they told me, Dave," said Kreevitch. "There was a note on a blotter in front of the cash register of some little food store in Red Lion or someplace. 'She's taking me to Wildwood,' he said."

Everybody was in Delio's for a council of war. Tommy was there, a free man; right after her operation Rochelle came to and made a statement that cleared his name, although Detective Cranmer said he thought she was lying. Saraleigh was there, mad as hell about Freddy. Randy Todd was there in hopes of recovering his Pontiac. Mother Grey, Jack Kreevitch, Mac Barrow, young Garrett Hudson, Schwartz, Danny, and Dave were all there as well, hoping to help somehow.

When they first came in, Horace Burkhardt had been at his usual table by the door, but when he saw Jack, he gave a snort and left. His pancakes and sausage were still sitting on his plate, the grease slowly congealing.

"I think we ought to go to Wildwood ourselves and try to find them," Saraleigh said.

"I've got to stay here," said Kreevitch. "I'm on duty, and anyhow I'm not sure how appropriate it would be for me to show up in Wildwood doing cop things. They have a perfectly good police force down there, you know. If it was them coming here, messing in our police business, I'm not sure I'd appreciate it."

"But we know what Dawn and Freddy look like," Tommy said. "They don't. And the more of us there are, the more likely we'll find them. We can spread out, search the whole town of Wildwood in no time."

"Dave?" Saraleigh said.

"I can't go down to Wildwood on a murder case with a big mob of civilians," said Dave. "But I'll go by myself. See you." He put the plastic top on his coffee, ripped a little triangle off so he could drink it in the car, and left.

"How about the rest of you?" said Tommy. "Will you come?"

Kreevitch said, "What are you going to do, rent a bus? Or go in a big car caravan? I can see it now, this long line of cars, stopping every ten miles so somebody can go to the bathroom."

"Caravan," Tommy said. "Right. I can get seven people in the Dodge."

"Didn't somebody tell you not to leave town?"

"Actually, no," he said. "Nobody told me nothin' like that. You aren't telling me not to leave town, are you, Jack? It's my daughter we're talking about. And my son." He cast a sidelong look at Saraleigh. She showed no reaction.

"No, no, go ahead," Kreevitch said.

"Seven people will fit in my van," Tommy said, and began to count heads. Randy Todd said he wanted to bring one of the Rottweilers, which took up another place. Finally Tommy agreed to carry Saraleigh, Garrett, Randy Todd, Randy's dog Shatzie, Danny Handleman, and Schwartz. Danny and Schwartz, as Freddy's official baby-sitters, demanded to be included.

"I'll take the Beemer," said Mac, "and Mother Vinnie can ride with me."

"Should we bring Towser?" Mother Grey said. "He might be able to—"

"I'd just as soon not have dogs in my car," Mac said. "If it's all the same to you."

"Where will we meet?" said Tommy.

"The Wildwood police station, as soon as we find out anything," Mother Grey said.

"Don't forget these." Tommy took a pack of wallet-sized pictures of Dawn out of his shirt pocket. "We had them made up the last time she ran away. You'll want to show them to people when you're searching for her." He handed them out to everyone. "All ready?"

"Let me go to the bathroom," said Danny.

"I have to get my dog," said Randy Todd.

"I'll call Marla," said Saraleigh. "See if she can keep the babies for the rest of the day. I bet we can get this all cleared up by tonight, before Ralphie gets home."

19

Mac drove sedately at first, keeping an eye out for Trooper Schoenwald and his ilk.

"Thanks for the ride," Mother Grey said. "I'm not sure the Nova could have made the journey to Wildwood. It needs the valves ground or something."

"Glad to do it," he said. "It looked pretty intense in that other car."

"You mean with the Rottweiler?"

"I meant with Tommy and Saraleigh."

"Ah. That." Who could tell what that relationship was all about? Freddy was eleven. Eleven years ago Tommy would already have been married to Rochelle, Dawn would have been three years old, Garrett in diapers, and Saraleigh would have been—what? Eighteen. Maybe they hadn't spoken to each other since. She thought of how they had all looked getting into the minivan at the curb in front of Delio's, two short-tempered former lovers, two adolescents, two certifiably disturbed young men, and an attack dog. It was like watching a group of vegetables climb into a pressure cooker and pull the lid down after themselves.

Many roads led down to Wildwood. Tommy Hudson and his stew of vigilantes set out on the interstate, but Mac, who explained that he had grown up in a small South Jersey town, preferred the back roads. He skirted Trenton by a bewildering series of detours, and then suddenly the soil and vegetation turned to sand, dwarf pine, scrub oak, and blueberry bushes, and they were streaking through the sparsely settled heart of the Jersey pine barrens. Mac had good tapes of ancient sacred music. His car's sound system was superb.

"So where is Paulsboro?" Mother Grey asked.

"Southwest of here."

"Your father was a minister there. Episcopal?"

"Baptist. It's a nice little town."

"Minister's children are said to be very wicked."

"That's me," he said, driving a little faster.

On a Sunday afternoon in high summer most of the shore traffic was coming the other way. Their side of the road was clear. As the needle crept up, large bugs began to splatter on the windshield, leaving iridescent streaks of red and yellow.

"You might want to slow down a bit," Mother Grey pointed out. "These roads are probably patrolled."

He gave her a look and eased up some.

"How did you get interested in music?" she said.

"I sang in my dad's church, and they thought I

was pretty good, so I got a scholarship to the American Boy Choir school in Princeton. So where did you grow up?"

"In Washington," said Mother Grey. "My grandmother brought me up after my parents were killed in an accident."

"That's rough."

"It was a long time ago." They changed the subject and talked about music. They listened to tapes, then to the radio.

The hourly news report featured the shootings in Fishersville and Rochelle Hudson's fight for life in the trauma center in Camden. Mother Grey was mentioned (the newscaster called her Reverend Grey). The newscaster played a tape, part of Mother Grey's passionate plea for people to turn in their guns.

"My word," she said. "I had no idea I sounded so convincing."

The newscaster went on to describe the resulting deluge of firearms on the steps of St. Bede's. "Even now the guns are still arriving."

"I certainly hope someone in authority is taking them away again," Mother Grey said. For the first time in days, she saw in her imagination the face of the Archdeacon contorted in scorn and loathing, not at graffiti this time but at the sight of a heap of sawed-off shotguns and Saturday-night specials decorating the church steps. When was he coming? Tuesday? Or was it—God help us!—tomorrow?

The news report said nothing of Dawn Hudson's flight or the kidnapping of Freddy. Evidently these facts had not been released to the press, still less the news that a crowd of semideranged vigilantes was converging on Wildwood.

Danny sat with Schwartz in the two seats in the middle of the minivan. Schwartz busied himself with a pad of paper and a map of Wildwood, making notes and calculations on it that seemingly had to do with military exercises. Garrett, Randy Todd, and the Rottweiler, Shatzie, occupied the very back. Shatzie hung over the back of Danny's seat and drooled down his neck.

Danny became more and more uncomfortable. Wasn't dog drool supposed to be a powerful allergen? Maybe it was cat drool. Whatever. In any case, he was sure he was going to be sick if he had to sit in this car much longer. If the dog drool didn't get him, the cigarette smoke would.

While Tommy Hudson drove, Saraleigh chain-smoked in the passenger seat in front. They went for a long time in silence, miles and miles. All you could hear was the dog panting and the sound of Schwartz's scratching pen.

"So," said Tommy finally. "Ralph treating you okay?"

"He treats me great," Saraleigh said. "Nice you're taking an interest." She didn't sound too grateful.

"Saraleigh, you know I always cared what happened to you. Don't pretend you didn't know that. Admit it, you never let me know what was going on."

"No point in it."

"What do you want from me?"

"Nothin' with a capital N."

Garrett began to whine. "Dad, I really, really have to go to the bathroom."

"I'll pull over, you can go in the bushes."

"With all those bugs and stuff? No way. I'll get poison ivy."

"There's a place up ahead," said Saraleigh. "I'm hungry anyhow. Let's stop."

"Yeah, let's," said Randy. "I could use something to eat myself."

Only one car was in the parking lot of the Bucket-O-Suds Inn when they got there, an electric blue 1963 Pontiac convertible. Randy said, "Dude, will you look at that shitty paint job. Mine is in a whole lot better shape than that."

"Let's hurry it up, troops," Tommy said. "We want to get in and out of this place as fast as we can. There's no time to lose." It was dark inside, all wood paneling, not one of your cheerful family places. They sold alcoholic beverages.

"It's a bar," said Danny.

"Go ahead in," said Schwartz. "I'm going to reconnoiter." Crouching low, he went around the back of the place.

Garrett rushed straight in and went to the men's room. Danny followed, looking around for a good table. He pretty much had his choice, since the only customers in there were two teenagers sitting in the corner booth eating hamburgers and drinking beer. The big round table in the middle of the room looked as though it would accommodate them all, but it had grease and crumbs on it. Maybe he could find a clean one.

There was something familiar about that girl.

Could it be—? He took out the picture of Dawn that Tommy had given him. No, no. That wasn't the same girl.

"Dawn!" said Tommy.

"Daddy!" Okay, so it was her.

He felt a shove; Saraleigh was pushing past him, past them all, grabbing the girl by the front of her skimpy shirt.

"Where is my son?" she was shouting.

"I don't know what you're talking about."

Smack! Saraleigh struck her across the face. The boy she was with jumped to his feet in amazement. Dawn hit back, and Danny thought sure the two of them were going to stand there and slug it out, when Tommy rushed forward and pinned Saraleigh's arms. Dawn took advantage of this to punch her in the nose; in retaliation, Saraleigh kicked her a good one. Dawn went sprawling across the table, but she was up in a moment, like a cat, and ducking behind the guy in the corner.

"Mariel," he said, "what is this? Who are these people?" Saraleigh, bleeding from the nose, struggled with Tommy, trying to get at the girl.

It was all very interesting to watch. Randy Todd was watching too, when he suddenly realized the meaning of what he was seeing.

"Hey. That *is* my car. Son of a *bitch*."

Dawn turned toward him, her eyes wild. "He's

the one I told you about, Guido, the one who raped me and kept me locked in a closet for three days."

"You pervert," Guido said with a curse, and made a dive for Randy.

"Get away from me, asshole." They started fighting, and then Saraleigh and Tommy started fighting too. Garrett came out of the bathroom.

"What the—?" Garrett said.

Through a small square window in the door to the kitchen, Danny could see a waitress and a cook huddled together, staring out with round eyes. Saraleigh gave up her struggles and collapsed in tears in Tommy's arms, whereupon Tommy started crying as well. The two of them stood there holding each other and sobbing. *What if Ralph should see them?* Danny wondered. *What would he think?* Maybe he would have an episode, have to go back to the hospital, a thing he hadn't done since he and Saraleigh were married. But no, what was Danny thinking of? Ralph was in Illinois driving a truck. As he thus reassured himself, an enormous tractor-trailer rolled into the parking lot with CHICAGO TRANS-PORT in huge letters on the trailer.

Randy was taking a pounding. Guido was small but vicious, obviously used to fighting.

"Garrett, go get Shatzie," Randy moaned. The boy went out.

Maybe I should do something, Danny thought, but he was darned if he could figure out what. The dog pushed the screen door open, came bounding in, and with a low growl seized Guido by the seat of his

227

pants. The howls and screams were something to hear.

The waitress was no longer in the little window. When he heard the sirens approaching, Danny figured she'd gone to phone the police. Meantime, Dawn . . . Where was Dawn? No matter, Schwartz was outside. He'd never let her get away.

Danny went to the screen door and looked out. A strange truck driver climbed down out of the rig—not Ralph, thank God. By looking between the wheels, Danny could see the electric blue convertible behind the trailer.

Then he saw a puff of exhaust come out of the back of the car, and heard the engine.

"Stop her!" he shouted. But she was gone again, roaring away in a cloud of gravel.

Schwartz came around the other side of the building.

"Schwartz! What were you doing?"

"Scouting the perimeter," Schwartz said. "Is there some problem?"

Dave Dogg didn't see Tommy's Caravan in the parking lot of the Bucket-O-Suds, or if he did, it didn't register; everybody and his brother drove those minivans nowadays. But he couldn't miss Randy Todd and his Rottweiler running down the road ahead of him.

He pulled over and called to the boy: "Get in, I'll give you a ride."

Randy got in. Tears were streaming through the

dust on his face. His dog scrambled into the back-seat.

"What's up?" Dave said. This kid hadn't cried at his own father's funeral.

"She took my car," he said. "She and this guy spray-painted it this disgusting color."

"I heard. Damned shame."

In Wildwood, Dave had traced Dawn to the Sleepy-Time Motel (Mariel Defarge, for Christ's sake) and found the heap of empty spray-paint cans outside the cabin she'd rented. He found witnesses who had seen the electric-blue convertible go back across the bridge over the bay. It must have been an amazing spectacle.

He followed. After that he went on instinct, bucking traffic until he came to a secondary road that looked as though it would beckon to someone who wanted to let a powerful car do what it could do. He guessed right.

"You saw her go this way?"

"Yeah. I don't know why I ran after her. I was hoping she'd run out of gas or something. You got a tissue?"

"Roll of paper towels on the floor," said Dave. With the ever-useful cellular phone, he called the state police and apprised them of the latest sighting of the fugitive.

"What about Freddy Kane?" Dave said to the kid. "Is he still in the car?"

"I don't know. We didn't see him."

* * *

Horace Burkhardt's last breakfast had been something of a failure, interrupted as it was by his not-to-be stepson and the rest of that rabble. It was time to try a last lunch. What would be good? Not pizza, it was too hard to chew. His uppers had been giving him trouble. How about that little French restaurant on Bridge Street? French food was mushy sometimes.

He had some cash. After he put an end to his troubles, he certainly wouldn't be needing it. He would get a bottle of wine at the liquor store, drink a last toast to the faithless Honey Kreevitch, another to his neglectful daughter and her swarthy fiancé, whoever he might be, and then he would have a tasty last meal.

Then he would go home and do it.

Randy had made his escape just in time from the madhouse that was the Bucket-O-Suds. No sooner had he and Shatzie disappeared over the horizon than the local police arrived and began to give everyone a hard time. Guido was bleeding from the rump, Saraleigh was bleeding from the nose, everyone except Garrett was in tears, and the officers seemed to have a great deal of difficulty understanding what was happening.

Two of them had come in one squad car to answer the waitress's call.

"Wisht I brought the video camera," one of the policemen muttered. "This would have been a natural for *True Stories of Real Cops.* We coulda been on national TV."

The cook, carrying a huge knife, came trembling out of the kitchen when he saw that the police were there. "Twenty years I been in business at this location," he said. "I never seen nothing like this."

"I want to press charges," Guido was saying. "I want to press charges of assault against everybody here and especially the dog. I want he should be put to sleep, destroyed."

"What dog?" said the first officer.

"Ma'am, did he strike you?" the second officer said to Saraleigh. "Did he hit you with a closed fist?" She only howled the louder. Danny had never seen her at a loss for words before.

Straight and flat went the road through the pine barrens. Far up ahead Dave Dogg could see the sun glinting off an electric-blue Pontiac convertible, or off what was left of the chrome after the sloppy paint job administered to the unhappy car by Dawn and her new friend.

Randy saw it too. "There she goes," he said. The Rottweiler growled low down in its throat. Dave sped up some. He was beginning to gain on her; he almost thought he could hear her stereo.

Way up ahead of the fleeing convertible, they could see flashing lights.

"There's the roadblock," said Dave. "We've got her now."

Dawn Hudson must have seen it too. Just ahead

of her a dirt road turned off to the right through a gap in the pine trees. When Dawn came to the turn-off, she hit the brakes, skidded into a sharp turn, and scratched away down the dirt road.

Dave followed her; he could do power slides too. Gaining on her faster now, they heard the radio going thoom, thoom, out of the speeding cloud of dust. After a long straight stretch that followed a deep ditch, the road formed a T-intersection at a big cranberry bog, neat rectangular fields of low bushes traversed and surrounded by dikes. Sand spewing from the back wheels, Dawn turned sharply right.

This time she didn't make it. The rear end began to drift, she lost control, and the car spun around in a circle. With a sickening crash the convertible plunged into a three-foot wall of earth.

Suddenly it was quiet, a profound silence broken only by the gentle hissing of the steam that jetted upward from the broken front of the Bonneville. Dave could hear the blood beating in his ears. Softly, Randy Todd cursed.

The slim form of Dawn Hudson popped out of the wrecked and silent car and fled across an earthen causeway through the bog. Dave jumped out and gave chase. She reached the other side; beyond lay the wood. *She can probably outrun me*, he thought, *but maybe* . . . As he formed a picture of himself overtaking her (an old athlete's trick), she stopped and turned to face him.

Right. She was still armed. Using both hands, she steadied the gun and shot him.

With a blinding pain in his head, he felt himself

falling. The last thing he was aware of was Randy Todd cursing and kicking his wrecked car.

"What's that up ahead?"

"Looks almost like a roadblock," said Mother Grey. Beyond the flashing lights, almost too far away to see, two cars were coming toward them.

As they approached the police roadblock, she could see in the distance first one car turning off the road, then the other.

"That second car looked green to me," she said.

"What second car?" Mac said.

"Those two cars, way up there. They turned off the road. I think the second one was Dave's car." Actually she knew it was Dave's car. She couldn't have said how; the green car was only a distant speck.

Mac glanced at her, and the look on his face was not full of warmth, but he said nothing. *Can't help it;* she thought, *I'm getting astral messages from Dave Dogg.*

He was even less pleased when the roadblock police pulled them over.

All the uniformed policemen she saw were beginning to look like the wretched Officer Schoenwald to Mother Grey, tall muscular fellows with glittering eyes, cryptofascists, even the black ones. These officers, however, simply glanced around inside Mac's car and waved them on.

"What do you suppose that was all about?" she said.

"Maybe they're looking for Dawn and Freddy," he said. "They knew they didn't have 'em when they saw us."

"I don't know," she said. "They didn't even check the trunk."

"Just as well."

"Which reminds me," she said, "You're going to have to think up a better story for them when they ask you why you quit baseball."

"How come?"

" 'Personal reasons.' It just sounds suspicious. I would pull you over and give you a ticket myself. How about 'My aged mother begged me to get into some other line of work'? Or 'The Lord came to me in a dream and told me to take up the pipe organ.' "

He laughed. "I'd get locked up for sure with a line like that."

"They turned here," she said. The two sets of skid marks leading into the side road were easy to see, black against gray.

"I guess we'll turn here too," he said. The side road stretched ahead of them long and straight through the scrubby growth until they came to the T-intersection at the end of it.

It was a strange picture that met their eyes when Mother Grey and Mac Barrow reached the cranberry bog. Dave Dogg's car was pulled up next to a wrecked electric-blue convertible. Randy Todd was leaning into the convertible's backseat, struggling mightily, as though he were engaged in some great effort. Mac parked the Beemer next to Dave's car, and they got out. They could hear the boy grunting.

"What are you doing?" Mac said.

"Trying to get the backseat out. Dawn took the keys. I can't get into the trunk."

"Freddy's not still in the trunk, is he?" Mother Grey said.

"Don't know."

"Let me help you," said Mac. "Are you okay in there, Freddy?"

There was no answer.

"Where's Dave?" Mother Grey said.

"Who?"

"Detective Dogg. That's his car parked over there."

"Oh, him," said the boy. "He's dead. Dawn shot him."

20

ave, dead? That couldn't be true. Could it? "Where is he?"

"Over there," Randy said. "On the dike." Someone was lying on the dike, sure enough, not moving, with a dark stain under his head.

Mother Grey was surprised that she could run as fast as she did. Dave's hands were cold, his lips almost white, but thank the Lord he was still breathing.

"Dave," she said.

"What?"

"Are you awake?"

"Yeah, I'm awake, but I feel really sick to my stomach. It gets worse if I move. Just let me lay here."

"Lie here," she corrected. Gently she brushed the matted hair back, revealing an ugly gash on the side of his head. But it was all hair and skin, no hole in the skull or any such thing. Surely a good sign.

"Ow, leave it alone," he said.

"I'll call you an ambulance."

"Good plan."

She took the cellular phone from his pocket and called the emergency people, telling them everything she knew. What had people done before cellular phones? Dave looked terrible, but maybe he'd be okay after all.

On the other side of the cranberry bog, Mac and Randy Todd gave a mighty heave and chucked the backseat of the convertible onto the sand. No one came out of the trunk. They bent over and looked in; they shook their heads; Mac shrugged. No Freddy.

Mother Grey waved to them, trying to indicate through body language that Dave was among the living. They came across the dike and joined her, Mac first, followed by Randy Todd and his dog.

"Nobody in the trunk," Mac said. "How's Dave?"

"Hanging on. I've called an ambulance."

"Dude. I thought sure he was dead," said Randy Todd. "You called the police too, right? I bet they'll shoot her. Did you see what she did to my car?"

Mother Grey realized that they probably would shoot her, a sick fourteen-year-old girl, since they knew she was armed and they knew she had shot, among others, two law-enforcement officers. Alone in a strange woods, Dawn Hudson didn't have a chance.

Unless some compassionate soul talked her out of there.

"I'm going to try to sit up," Dave said.

"Don't," she said. "Just be still."

"Sometimes with a head injury it's better if you elevate it," Dave said. "I'm sure it's—ugh!—I'm sure it's no worse than a concussion."

"How do you know?" she asked. "You never get hurt on the job."

He was up on one elbow, but he looked pretty green.

"All right, then, let me hold you." She knelt beside him, supporting his head; he relaxed his upper body against her. The wound was hardly bleeding anymore.

"Dave, do you know where Freddy is?" Mac asked.

"No," Dave said. "He could be anywhere. Dawn could have left him in Wildwood, or she could have dumped him by the side of the road someplace."

"She was with this guy Guido," said Randy Todd. "Maybe he knows where Freddy is. We ought to go back to the bar and ask him."

"What bar?"

"The Bucket-O-Suds. We stopped to eat, and that's where we found them. But no Freddy."

"Do you think Guido is still in the bar?" said Mac.

"We can go and see," said Randy Todd. "If you want to. If not, we can head back to Wildwood and search for Freddy."

"You two go ahead," said Mother Grey. "I can stay with Dave till the ambulance gets here, then drive his car back."

"Good, let's go," said Randy Todd. "C'mon, Shatzie."

Mac looked at the boy, then at the large smelly dog, and then back at Mother Grey, holding Dave. He seemed uncomfortable, but he said, "Okay." Not until later did she remember how much he hated having dogs in his car.

"Who says you can drive my car?" said the corpse.

She kissed his fingers. "Please?"

"Okay. The keys are in my pants."

"They will shoot her, won't they?" she said softly. That poor psychotic girl was as good as dead. Unless someone could persuade her to give herself up.

"I know what you're thinking," said Dave.

"You always do," she said. "But I'm a trained counselor, Dave. We have procedures for crises. I'll be careful. I would never put myself in harm's way."

"Just do me one favor. There's a bulletproof vest in my trunk. Promise me you'll put it on."

"I promise," she said. She fished out his car keys. Then having made her plan, she sat and waited, holding his head and brushing the mosquitoes off him.

The state police arrived about the same time as the ambulance. Two officers came and talked to Dave. "The helicopter is coming," one of them said. "We're going to wait for that before we go after her. She can't get far on foot." The policemen continued to gather, some in SWAT gear, but they did not yet go into the woods.

On the grounds that, since Dave had fallen down when the bullet struck him, he might have injured his spine somehow, the paramedics strapped him to a board to get him into the ambulance. He complained the whole time they were doing it. He kept saying he felt fine, better and better, he was sure he was only lightly concussed, and then he threw up. Away they went into the steamy afternoon.

The police were still waiting for their helicopter backup when Mother Grey set out into the interior of the pine barrens, hot on the trail of an armed murderess. Everyone was looking up, searching the skies for the 'copter; nobody saw Mother Grey take the bulletproof vest from Dave's trunk, or noticed her leaving. The woods were hot, close, and insect-infested, but the smell of the pines was pleasant.

When Dawn Hudson took off into the woods, it had not been with any idea of evading a sharp-eyed tracker. She had broken branches, left footprints, stopped to light cigarettes, and dropped the matches. In the moist, still air of the pines Mother Grey was able to follow her almost by scent alone, from her heavy perfume and the smoke of her cigarettes, even with a half-hour start.

Her friend Deacon Deedee Gilchrist would have been proud of her. Cutting sign, Deedee called it. Deedee had learned all about it from the works of Louis L'Amour. Thinking about that writer of noble westerns caused Mother Grey to think about coffee, and then to want some. It struck her that she had missed her lunch.

Here the girl had crossed a stream, deep and wide enough for canoeing. *Someday I'll come back here*, thought Mother Grey. *When I've no reason to fear for my life.* These wild and dwarfish woods would be a pleasant place to hike. The songs of birds, the rustling of small animals. A patch of wild blueberries that would be ripe in another month. The woods showed signs of other humans passing, and of hunters, though hunting season wasn't until fall. There were platforms built in the occasional tall trees, a duck blind by the pond.

The cigarette reek grew stronger. Maybe Dawn was hiding up in one of these hunter's platforms, or crouched in a duck blind, waiting for a clear shot at Mother Grey. *Why wouldn't she shoot me? She's shot everybody else, for heaven's sake.* At least she wouldn't get her in the back, if her back was what she aimed for. The vest, though heavy and hot, gave a feeling of safety, like the protective embrace of Dave Dogg himself.

But would the willful teenager have the foresight to hide herself beside the trail and ambush pursuers? No, she would be more likely to seek comfort somewhere, to stop someplace and have her lunch, since she hadn't had any more time to eat that day than Mother Grey. A hunting lodge or a fishing camp, someplace that might have a table in it, maybe canned goods stored from season to season. That would be where she would go.

Sure enough, over the next rise was the old abandoned house.

The house had a terrifying familiarity: the weathered cedar siding, the shotgun-pitted window frames, the front door with its peeling blue paint hanging open at just that precise angle. For a moment she thought it was the house of her nightmares, the place where the horrors happened, but she thought, *That can't be, I've never been in the pines before.* The prototype for the nightmare house had to be in Virginia or Maryland, a house she had visited as a child on some occasion that she couldn't quite remember. This house was very similar, though, of a similar vintage and design, similarly neglected, similarly abused, similarly decayed.

She even knew what it would smell like when she stepped inside: mouse droppings, water-damaged plaster, and rotted wood.

Also pickles and ketchup.

Dawn was sitting on the windowsill having a solitary picnic with the remains of her lunch.

"Nice vest," Dawn said. "But I can always shoot you in the head, you know." Her face was hideous with streaming mascara; her hair had electric-blue paint in it.

"I know," said Mother Grey.

"Why did you come here?"

"Why do you think?"

"Because you're stupid," Dawn said.

"Listen to me. Your mother isn't dead."

"She's not?"

"They took her to the hospital. She's expected to pull through."

"She was trying to keep me and Randy apart."

"Is that why you shot her?"

"I shot her because she was an alcoholic slut," she said. "I couldn't take it anymore. She was destroying my father."

"Are you telling me sick people deserve death?"

"Shut up! Shut up! You don't know anything! Was your mother a drunk? You know nothing!"

"My mother died when I was three," said Mother Grey.

"You were lucky. Your father was lucky."

"My father was killed in the same accident."

"I suppose you expect me to feel sorry for you." The last crumbs of hamburger were gone. She wiped her mouth with the back of her hand.

"And what about the others?" said Mother Grey.

"What others?"

"Bunker Todd. George Pitts, the ranger."

"What about them?"

"You killed them, didn't you?"

She rolled her eyes—the bad girls always roll their eyes—and reached into her bag. Mother Grey thought, *Here it comes, she's going to try to murder me.* But instead of the gun she pulled out a pack of cigarettes and a lighter, lit up, and started puffing.

"They were perverts," she said. "Both of them. As for my mother—she had this great plan. When Mr. Todd bought the ball field, she was going to get this huge commission and leave my father."

"And so . . ." Mother Grey prompted.

"Her scheme involved sleeping with him. Are you ready for that? She was cheating on my father with this man."

"So you . . ."

"She had this big fight with my father one night. She promised him, *promised him* that she wouldn't see Bunker Todd anymore."

"But instead—"

"I followed her to see whether she would keep her word. Once I had a gun, I could make sure of it, you see?"

"I think so."

"Naturally she went straight to him."

"Where was Randy Todd while all this was going on?"

"I needed his car. When I knew what my mother was doing, I sent him home."

"What was she doing?"

"I told you. Talking to Bunker Todd."

"I see."

"So as soon as she went away again, I shot him. It was kind of an interesting challenge, he was moving and everything, rolling along in his little golf cart, and still I managed to get him right between the eyes. Or I think I did. I called his name, and he turned toward me. Well, maybe he slowed down a little. Maybe it wasn't such a difficult shot. You know, I threw that gun away in the sewer, but somehow it got back in my house. Isn't that funny?"

"What about the park ranger?"

"What park ranger?"

"George Pitts. The ranger. You shot him on the canal bank, didn't you?"

"Oh, yeah." She put the cigarette to her lips, inhaled deeply, and let a long stream of smoke out through her nose. "Him. So weird. I had to shoot him twice, the first time I didn't get him, he was still moving."

"Why, Dawn?"

"He saw me hiding in the bushes the day Bunker Todd was shot."

"He never said anything. Did you think he knew you were the killer?"

"He would have figured it out as soon as somebody talked to him. He was a pervert but he wasn't stupid."

"What makes you think he was a pervert?"

"He was always watching me." She flipped the cigarette through the glassless window. "So why did you follow me here?"

"I came here to warn you, Dawn. You shot two law-enforcement officers."

"So?"

"You started something that won't be stopped until you give yourself up or they kill you."

"What are you trying to say?"

"My dear child, I'm trying to tell you that you are marked for death. If you come with me now, I can save you. But you have to tell me where you left Freddy."

"Freddy? He went home. I don't know where he is."

"Tell me," she insisted.

"We left him in Wildwood with five rolls of quarters. He's playing a video game."

More lies. What Mother Grey needed to know was what tree she had tied him to, or what closet she had locked him in. "If you don't tell me what you did with him, I'm going to walk out of here alone. Then all those policemen will come in here after you, and one of them will shoot you."

"You wouldn't do that."

"Maybe all of them will shoot you," Mother Grey said. "In any case, it won't be pleasant. Do you want to get out of here alive?"

This time she really took the revolver out of the bag. "Do you?"

"I'm not going to play hostage to you, Dawn. Shoot me or don't shoot me, I'm not going to do it. The only chance you have is to put down that gun and tell me where I can find Freddy." A wisp of smoke curled up outside the window.

"He's such a little liar," Dawn said, lighting another cigarette. "He was trying to tell me that we're related, that my father is his father too."

"You might want to talk to your father about that."

"What?"

"I think it might be true."

If Mother Grey wanted the girl off-balance, she got her wish then. She stood up, seeming quite unable to get her breath or indeed to close her mouth. But before Mother Grey could think of some way to take advantage of her agitation, she brought the gun up and fired.

Of the original parties to the melee at the Bucket-O-Suds, four were left. An ambulance had come for Guido, whose bottom was declared by the police officers to be severely chewed. Another ambulance came and took Saraleigh away, even though she protested and howled the whole time that it was only a bloody nose, she'd had a hundred of 'em and didn't want to go to no friggin' hospital. No sooner were they out of sight than Mac Barrow and Randy Todd stuck their heads in, looking for Guido or some news of Freddy.

When they found that Guido was not there, they rushed out again, saying they were going to look for Freddy in Wildwood. No one was left at Bucket-O-Suds but the trucker, placidly eating his meat loaf at the counter, the original waitress and cook, Danny, Schwartz, Tommy, and Garrett. Tommy invited Danny and Schwartz to order a meal, it was on him. They took a table by the window.

Seeing that the most violent members of the group seemed to be gone, the waitress came out from behind the counter. "Are you folks ready to order?" Danny was still perusing the menu, looking for something healthful.

"What's good today?" Tommy said.

Then Danny looked up and saw it, coming in low over the pines. "The black helicopter is here."

"The meat loaf is today's chef special."

"Damn," said Schwartz. "And me without my gun. Whatever happened to that, anyhow, Danny?"

"I dunno," Danny said.

"I'll have a hamburger," said Garrett. "And a Sprite."

"You had it," Schwartz said.

"I did?" Danny said.

"Let me have the meat loaf and a cup of coffee," Tommy said.

"You had it," Schwartz said. "What did you do with it?"

"Nothing," Danny said.

"Well, where is it?" Schwartz said.

"I gave it to that old guy Horace Burkhardt."

"You did what?" Schwartz said.

"Schwartz, you're crazy and you know it. The last thing you need is a gun."

"You did *what*?"

"For instance, right now if you had a gun, you'd be out there blazing away at that helicopter."

"Yes!"

"But from where I'm sitting, I can see there are no UN soldiers in it. It's a police helicopter," Danny said.

"Sure it is. They all are. You moron," said Schwartz. "You mindless dupe."

"Are you gentlemen ready to order?" the waitress asked. All this time the helicopter noise was growing ever louder.

"It's coming down in the parking lot," said Danny.

"They've come to get me," said Schwartz. "Maybe I can hit it with a rock or something. Where's that cook? He had a big knife, as I recall."

"Perhaps I should come back when you're ready," said the waitress, backing away a step or two.

"Just get them each a hamburger and a root beer," said Tommy. "Medium rare." She wrote it down and rushed for the kitchen.

"Make mine well done," Danny called after her. You could get very bad things from undercooked meat. Especially in restaurants. The helicopter was on the ground now. "Look, someone's getting out. It's—"

"It's Uncle Jack," said Garrett. "Good."

Jack Kreevitch came in the door wearing his bicycle-cop outfit, the black shorts with the T-shirt that said POLICE across the back. He glanced around until his eyes grew accustomed to the gloom. The trucker at the counter was staring again. He must have been hard up for entertainment.

"Come on, Tommy, we need you," Kreevitch said. "We think we've found out where she is, and we want you to get her out of there before some trigger-happy law officer blows her away."

"Can I come?" Garrett said.

" 'Fraid not, little buddy. There's only room for one more in the 'copter. Stay here, we'll be back for you."

So Danny had to pay for the lunches.

Kreevitch was completely delighted with the state police helicopter. It was the last word in pursuit craft, with a built-in infrared camera and a screen where your fugitive appeared as a big red hot spot. As they flew along, the technician told him many an interesting story of captures the police had made using the device. It could find guys hiding under porches and all kinds of places; you could use it to count men in a warehouse. All they needed to be was warm and breathing.

"There it is," the pilot said. The smoke that rose

from the yard could be seen for quite a distance, but now the house itself was visible to the naked eye among the trees. On the screen the police officers moving to surround it showed as wiggly shapes, red and orange with outlines of blue.

"What's burning?" said Tommy.

"Your daughter appears to have set fire to the yard. That's how we found the place, by the smoke."

"Figures," said Tommy.

Slowly they cruised over the house. The brushfire passed across the infrared device's screen in a riot of orange and yellow.

"Can you see whether she's inside?" said Tommy.

"Sure can. See there?" A hot area roughly the shape of Dawn was moving around in what might have been the front room. But wait. Another area, somewhat less hot, showed toward the back of the house. It was not moving.

"Who the hell is that?" said Tommy.

"Dunno. Some of the guys said they saw this woman go into the woods after the girl, they weren't sure who it was, maybe some clergywoman. Could be her."

Kreevitch had a cold feeling in the pit of his stomach. The smoke was getting thicker.

"That fire isn't going to spread to the house, is it?" said Tommy.

"Might. Can't tell. We'll put this bird down on the other side of the house from the fire."

Back and forth, back and forth, the moving Dawn-shape continued to prowl the screen, ever closer to the shape that was not moving.

"Put it down now, can't you?" said Tommy. "I want to get her the hell out of there."

"Wait," said the technician.

Closer, closer. Then as they watched, the immobile shape suddenly heated up visibly, sprang toward the moving shape, and merged with it. Struggling? Or hugging? Who the hell knew? Mother Grey was, after all, a Christian woman.

The last supper of Horace was very good indeed, but so rich and abundant that he was unable to finish the dessert he ordered.

"Can I wrap it for you, sir?" the waitress offered.

"No, thanks," said Horace. "I don't expect to live long enough to eat it."

"Oh," she said. "I'm so sorry." She brought him the check; when he figured the tip at fifteen percent, it seemed much too high for a tip, so he just left her a five-dollar bill with what he owed for the meal and headed on home. It was getting to be time.

One bullet for Bunker Todd, two for the park ranger, two for Rochelle; that made five. Perhaps one chamber empty for safety. Mother Grey knew the gun Dawn was brandishing was a nine-shooter; her father had left her one just like it. The bullet that grazed Dave made six, the one that hit Mother Grey's bulletproof vest made seven. So one or two more bullets left, presuming Dawn hadn't bothered to reload, or one or none, if she had shot poor Freddy.

The trick would be to get her to fire twice more and then rush her.

When the bullet hit the vest, Mother Grey had gone reeling backward through the door to the kitchen. She knew the layout of this place; it was the same as the other, and hadn't she dreamed of it a hundred times? For instance, on the other side of this short door, there were backstairs leading upward. Even without knowing the design of the house, she could see that from the riser and the lip of the first step sticking out under the door. Quietly she opened it and went up, pulling the door closed behind her.

"Mother Grey!"

She kept very still.

"Mother Grey, come out! I won't hurt you. I want to talk."

Go ahead and talk. Debris littered the floor of the upstairs hall. Mother Grey almost made noise stumbling over a small block of wood. Then she thought, *Ah. The old tricks are the best.* She picked it up.

At the head of the stairs, she could look down and see Dawn creeping toward the kitchen door, holding the gun in front of her with both hands.

And here's the pitch. The block of wood bounced off the window frame and fell behind an old wrecked chair. Dawn whirled and fired at the sound. One bullet left. Or no bullets, if Freddy . . .

Smoke.

Mother Grey tripped and fell backward, making a horrendous racket.

"I know you're up there!" Dawn said. "You're

dead!" The girl came charging up the stairs, gun outstretched. Mother Grey by this time had ducked into the last bedroom and latched the door. The wallpaper was different. She remembered thin brown stripes on a cream background with bouquets of brown flowers, not this silly pattern of pink bears. Her grandmother was there. The mouse smell was bringing the memory into focus—it had to do with property in Maryland, an old farmhouse. If she lived through this adventure, she would work on remembering. Not now.

Walking up and down, up and down, Dawn searched the second floor. Mother Grey stood very still.

The smoke grew thicker.

Finally the girl stopped by the door to the last bedroom. Mother Grey couldn't keep herself from sneezing.

"You're dead!" Dawn cried, and fired into the wall.

And that was how Dawn's last bullet—always presuming she hadn't reloaded—buried itself harmlessly in the joist. She must have thought she was using a Dirty Harry gun, a .357 Magnum; she must have expected to blow a big hole in the wall the way they did it in the movies. But it was only a .22.

Mother Grey came out of the bedroom in a rush and jumped the girl, knocking her down in the dust. They struggled for the pistol. Mother Grey got it away from her.

Smoke. Thicker and thicker, rolling up the front stairs. "Come on, Dawn," she said, "we've got to get out of here." Keeping her arm around the girl she led her down the back way and toward the kitchen door. Flames flickered in the front room; the house was doomed.

The back door burst open.

"Uncle Jack!" Sure enough, it was Kreevitch. He pulled them out through the door and into the yard.

"Daddy!"

"Sugar babe." The two embraced. Mother Grey, meanwhile, examined the revolver and found that there were four more shots left in it. So Dawn had reloaded after all. *Oh, well.*

"Daddy, it isn't true about Freddy, is it? What they said. You aren't really his father?"

"Well . . . er . . . ah . . ."

"That's *disgusting*!"

"Honey, when you're older, you'll understand better. There are some things—"

"That little *snot*! I should have killed him when I had the chance!"

INSERT QUARTER TO CONTINUE GAME!

With numb fingers Freddy fished in his pocket, but there were no more quarters.

The figures on the screen stood frozen in attitudes of murderous hatred. The message began to flash: INSERT QUARTER NOW TO CONTINUE GAME! 5 . . . 4 . . . 3 . . .

No more quarters. The last roll was gone.

2 . . . 1 . . .

Maybe it was just as well. There was a cramp in

his hand; he was hungry, thirsty, and sluggish from lack of sleep. Maybe it was time to quit. Maybe man was not meant to reach the twenty-seventh level of Bloody Death.

He turned away from the game. Without a backward glance he stepped out of the dark noisy arcade into the afternoon sunlight of the Wildwood boardwalk. Somewhere around here there would be a policeman. It was time to find him now.

21

On Monday morning, hunger and a broken coffeemaker drove Mother Grey to Delio's. It was one of those steamy mornings that promises a hot day. She walked briskly, thinking, *I'll take this much exercise, anyhow.* Then later if it got too hot, she wouldn't have to feel guilty about not moving.

Freddy was home; Mac and Randy Todd had found him running the streets of Wildwood. Dawn was locked up in the pokey. Rochelle, making a steady recovery, stuck to her story of how it was her daughter who shot her.

Dave Dogg hadn't even been admitted to the hospital, so superficial was the wound the girl had dealt him; all they did with him in the emergency room was check him for broken bones and make him lie down for three hours. Mother Grey picked him up at the hospital in Toms River; he let her off in Fishersville and drove himself home to Felicia.

So now there was nothing to worry about except the forthcoming visit of the Archdeacon and his minions, scheduled for tomorrow, and the immediate necessity of coffee. She walked a little faster. Horace Burkhardt came hobbling the other way, pancake crumbs and sausage grease all over the front of his shirt.

"Good morning, Horace. Beautiful day, isn't it?"

"Good-bye, Mother Grey. You, at least, I have been pleased to know. Don't forget what we agreed about my funeral."

"And a very nice day to you," she said. Oh, how she needed her coffee. Maybe later on she would look in on the old plaster, see what it was that was ailing him this time.

Jack Kreevitch was sitting at a table in Delio's when she came in, eating eggs and bacon, poring over a stack of papers.

"Hello, Jack," she said. "What are you doing?"

"Looking to see if we got all the guns." He held up a fat stack of papers. "This is the list of the ones that were brought to St. Bede's, descriptions and serial numbers."

"My word." Two inches thick. Even reduced to one short description per gun, the mound of artillery took up a lot of space.

"And these are the guns stolen from Bunker Todd's house." A single sheet of paper, five entries on it, three crossed off. "This is the one Dave has," he said, "this is the one you took from Dawn, this one turned up on the church steps. We're still missing the little Ruger revolver and the automatic."

"You'll find them on the other list, though, don't you think?"

"I've been over it once and didn't find them. I'm just double-checking." He was keeping his place with his thumb.

"How's Tommy doing?"

"They let him back in last night; he doesn't have to stay with me and Marla."

"Good. How are his spirits?"

"He's not too thrilled about Dawn, but I guess he's glad he isn't in jail. And he's happy that Rochelle wasn't hurt any worse. They may let her go home at the end of next week. My mom is going to keep house for Tommy and Garrett until Rochelle is all better."

"Dawn won't be coming home, will she?"

Kreevitch shook his head. "I don't think they're going to let Dawn out anytime soon. Probably they'll just lock her up in a mental hospital, but right now she's sharing a cell in the Blue Roof Hotel with some bad ladies."

As Mother Grey ordered coffee and selected a cranberry muffin, a woman walked in wearing a Mexican peasant skirt and a souvenir straw hat. It was Horace Burkhardt's daughter, tanned and rested-looking.

"Allison!" Mother Grey called. "So good to see you back!" Never had welcome been more heartfelt. *Now, how can I tactfully find out her last name, for the next time I need to find her?*

"Oh, hi, Mother Grey."

"When did you get in?" *Could you write your*

name for me? I'm not certain how to spell it. Why, certainly, she says, and she writes, S-m-i-t-h.

"Late last night on the red-eye. I haven't even been to see my dad yet. How's he been? Okay?"

"More or less. He thinks you're married to a Mexican citizen by now," Mother Grey said. *I guess then your name would be Garcia or something, rather than . . .*

"Oh, yeah, right. I went out with a guy one night in Cancún. Actually he was Canadian, and he went home to Toronto the next day."

"You wouldn't be suggesting that your dad likes to exaggerate, would you, Ms. Krumm?" Kreevitch said.

"My dad? Never."

Krumm. As Mother Grey wrote it down surreptitiously in her pocket organizer, Freddy Kane and Danny Handleman came in and asked Rose de Leo to give them half a dozen chocolate doughnuts.

"How ya doin', Fred?" Kreevitch said.

"Hi, Uncle Jack," Freddy said with a wicked grin. *Uncle Jack? Wait a minute, if Tommy is his father, does that make Rochelle his stepmother? If so, is Jack his stepuncle? Or . . . Oh, never mind.*

"Did Horace give you the gun?" Danny asked Mother Grey.

"What gun?" she said.

"I gave him this gun that Schwartz had. I gave it to him on Saturday. He said he was going to give it to you."

"I don't know," she said. "I guess he left it on the

church steps with the others. We found hundreds of guns there."

"You don't think he kept it, do you?" Danny said. "I've been thinking about it, and I'm not sure I liked the look on his face when I gave it to him."

"Kept it?" *What would Horace want with a gun?*

"What would my dad want with a gun?" Allison said.

"What are you guys going to do with all those doughnuts?" Kreevitch asked.

"Eat 'em. Schwartz sent us to get treats," Freddy said.

"We're having a little party to celebrate," Danny said. "Frank got out of the hospital today."

"That's wonderful," Mother Grey said.

"Also Ralph came home from Illinois last night," Freddy said.

"Even better."

"My mom says he found us a house. We might move out there. Then he can be home three nights a week."

Oh, no! The Voercker-Kane household was ten percent of her congregation. Besides, she was very fond of them all. "We would miss you so much," Mother Grey said.

"I'd miss you too, Mother Vinnie. And I'd have to go to a new school and make all new friends. But you know what?"

"What?"

"Rex Perskie would never, never find us again."

"I guess that's true. Too bad we can't ship him to Illinois, and the rest of you stay here."

"Amen," muttered Kreevitch.

"My mom says she likes the idea of moving, making a new start. Ralph says I can have a puppy if we move."

"What kind of dog do you want?" she said.

"A real big one. By the way, somebody left another gun on the church steps," Freddy said.

"They did?"

"Yes, I saw it on my way over here. I think it's a Ruger double-action twenty-two-caliber revolver."

Danny paid for the doughnuts, and Freddy picked up the paper bag. When they went out the door Freddy was whistling.

Jack Kreevitch checked his short list. "Double-action Ruger revolver," he said. "All *right*." He collected his papers. As he stood up to go, a handsome woman in late middle age, tanned and plump, her hair dyed champagne blond, sailed into the coffee shop and accosted him. "Jackie."

"Hi, Mom," he said.

"I want you to see this letter I got from that old fool Horace. He left it in Rochelle and Tommy's mailbox for me." She held it out; it was hand-scrawled on a page of yellow legal paper. Mother Grey and Allison crowded around to read it.

The note was of the good-bye-forever-it's-all-your-fault variety, and Mother Grey suddenly remembered the wild remarks Horace had directed at her when she was on her way to get breakfast.

"He's going to shoot himself." The words were out of her mouth before she realized she was saying them. Oh, why hadn't she listened to the old codger?

261

She could have had him safely in the medical center by now.

Allison and Jack Kreevitch were first out the door, followed by Honey and then Mother Grey, gaining fast. Horace's house was only two and a half blocks from the coffee shop. Maybe they could get there in time to stop him.

Then they heard the shot.

A wisp of gunpowder drifted from the open window of Horace's motor home. They found him in the reclining driver's seat, the place where he liked best to be. His face was white. His right arm hung down, the hand clasping a black automatic. There was a small bloodstain on his shirt.

"My God! Daddy!"

"I'm dead," he said. Yet another of Horace's exaggerations. Jack Kreevitch examined him.

"Get away from me, you snake," Horace mumbled.

"Is he—will he be okay?" Allison said.

"He seems to be fine, all things considered," said Kreevitch as he took the gun away from him. "Your father appears to have shot himself in the chest with a twenty-two-caliber piece of soap. It tore his shirt and gave him a slight wound, nothing life-threatening."

Yet another suicide note lay on the dashboard. Allison read it. "This is all nonsense," she said. "Daddy, how could you say these things? I never did any of—and how could you do this?" She crumpled the note and leaned her head on the doorjamb. "I think I'm going to need counseling."

Mother Grey put her arm around her. "Come see me in my office this afternoon at two," she said.

"Thought I was dead," said Horace. "What happened?"

Kreevitch had the gun apart and was examining the clip. "Your gun was loaded with soap," he said. "Where the hell did you get this thing, Horace? Did Danny give you this?"

"Soap?" the old man said.

"Meantime," said Mother Grey, "we'll get him into the County Medical Center. I've been all through this before with Ralph. They'll put him on a suicide watch and start him on medication. It'll be okay." Since Frank was out, there was certain to be a bed available in the mental health ward.

"Allison and I can drive him to the hospital," said Honey. "Come with us, Horace."

"What's this?" Horace said. "You're taking me where?"

"To the medical center," said Honey. "In my car."

"Unless you think you need to be tied to a gurney," said Allison. He stood up and felt himself.

"Not dead," he said. "Damn."

"I'll come and visit you, Horace," said Mother Grey, taking his hand and patting it.

Kreevitch, his face turned away from them all, was leaning on Horace's built-in dining table. His shoulders were quivering.

"Soap," he said.

* * *

The following Saturday afternoon found Mother Grey in a festive mood. Once again the Archdeacon had come and gone without closing the church. Tomorrow's sermon was written. A knock sounded at the front door, Towser barked hysterically, and there on the doorstep stood Dave Dogg, his hair combed, reeking of aftershave. *What, no flowers?* "Come in," she said.

"I just thought I'd come by and give you the news in person," he said. "We caught the kid who shot the Seven-Eleven clerk."

"Wonderful."

"A sixteen-year-old crack addict from Hanover Street. One of his little friends ratted on him, and his prints were on the gun. So he confessed. We don't need any more evidence than that. His lawyer is doing a plea-bargain thing."

"How's your head?" She couldn't even see the wound. It must be under his hair. The shirt she had worn when she held him as he lay bleeding was in the ragbag now; she had put it there after his blood refused to come out in the wash.

"Head's fine. Sort of. It was just a concussion, basically. They gave me a CAT scan, nothing wrong, take these pills when you get a headache. The city paid for it. I'll probably have a scar, but only when I finish going bald."

"You were lucky."

"Lucky. Yeah. I have a headache that won't quit, my head feels like it's full of rat fur, and the doctor says there's nothing I can do about it except wait for it to go away. If I was really lucky, she would have missed me."

"You could have been killed, and you know it."

"Actually I do know it. I've been doing some thinking."

"So your Seven-Eleven killer confessed," she said. "Does this mean you won't need to chase the Fishersville boys anymore?"

"The Fishersville gun-heist gang is off the hook, as far as Trenton Homicide is concerned. Jack Kree-vitch will have to deal with them."

"I'm sure he can handle it. My, you smell nice," she said. "Cologne. Is that a present from Felicia?"

"No. Felicia won't be giving me any more presents. We've decided to . . . You're looking kind of dressed up yourself. Is there some occasion?"

"I have a date."

"You have a date."

"I'm going to a concert with Mac Barrow."

It took him a moment to digest this information. "Oh, yeah, the concert. I heard about that. Bruce Springsteen is going to be at the Spectrum, right? How did Mac get tickets? Weren't they all sold out?"

"Actually, we're going to Carnegie Hall to hear a string quartet," she said. Mac had gotten them great seats where she could get a good look at the cellist's hands, study his technique.

"Oh," said Dave. "So, you and the ball player, huh?"

"I don't know about *that*, but I do need a little time away from Fishersville now and then. Apart from perilous adventures in the pines. You know, something civilized."

"You look great in that dress," he said.

"Got it at the thrift shop," she said. "It's twenty years old or so, but I understand they're back in style." Mac's car drove up. "Ah, here he is now." A man of iron guts, Mac planned to drive his beloved Beemer to Manhattan, park it there somewhere, and walk away from it, and all to show her a good time. She was moved and impressed by this.

He got out of the car, wearing not baseball clothes but a suit and tie, and came up the walk. He looked very nice.

"Damn," said Dave. "Your date looks like Denzel Washington."

"Who?"

"Movie star. But I was forgetting, you never go to the movies. Have a good time," Dave said.

"Thanks," she said. "I think I will."